Abyssinia

I dedicate this book to all those who fought the evils of fascism, communism, National Socialism, warlordism, and all the other "...isms" that debase the human soul through an overarching, totalitarian government.

A Novel By
Captain S. Martin Shelton, USNR (ret.)

Lamplight Press

acknowledgements

Danielle Harman Acee for her sterling formatting of this text for publication and outstanding guidance on publication and promotion of this novel

Doug Brown for his superior cover art

K. C. Francis for her eagle-eye editing

Mindy Reed for her outstanding editing of this narrative

Chris R. Sterling (*nom de guerre*) for his/her realistic contributions to the intelligence sequences in this narrative

Bradley Wilson from Yellow Bird Editors for his superior content editing

i

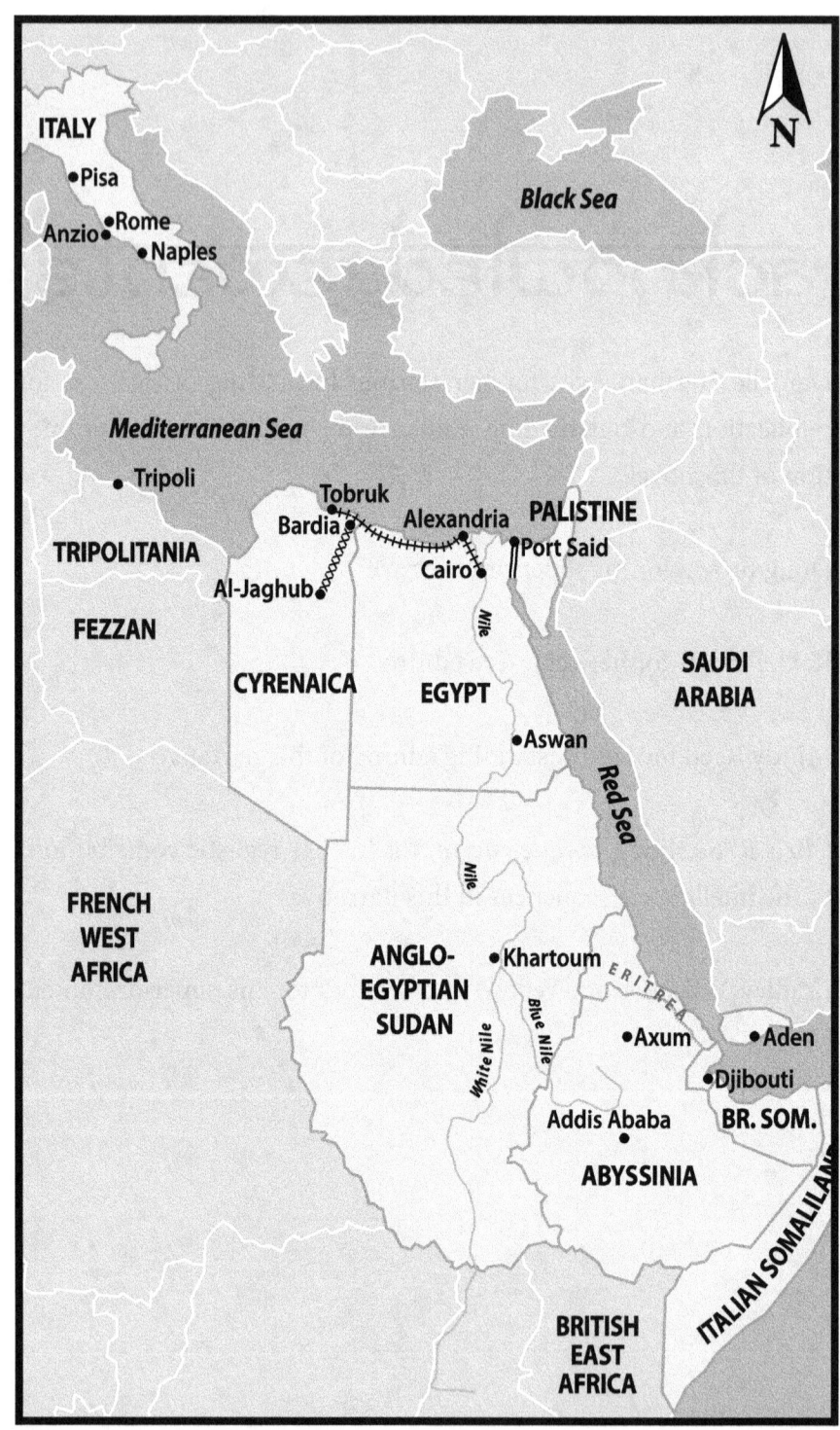

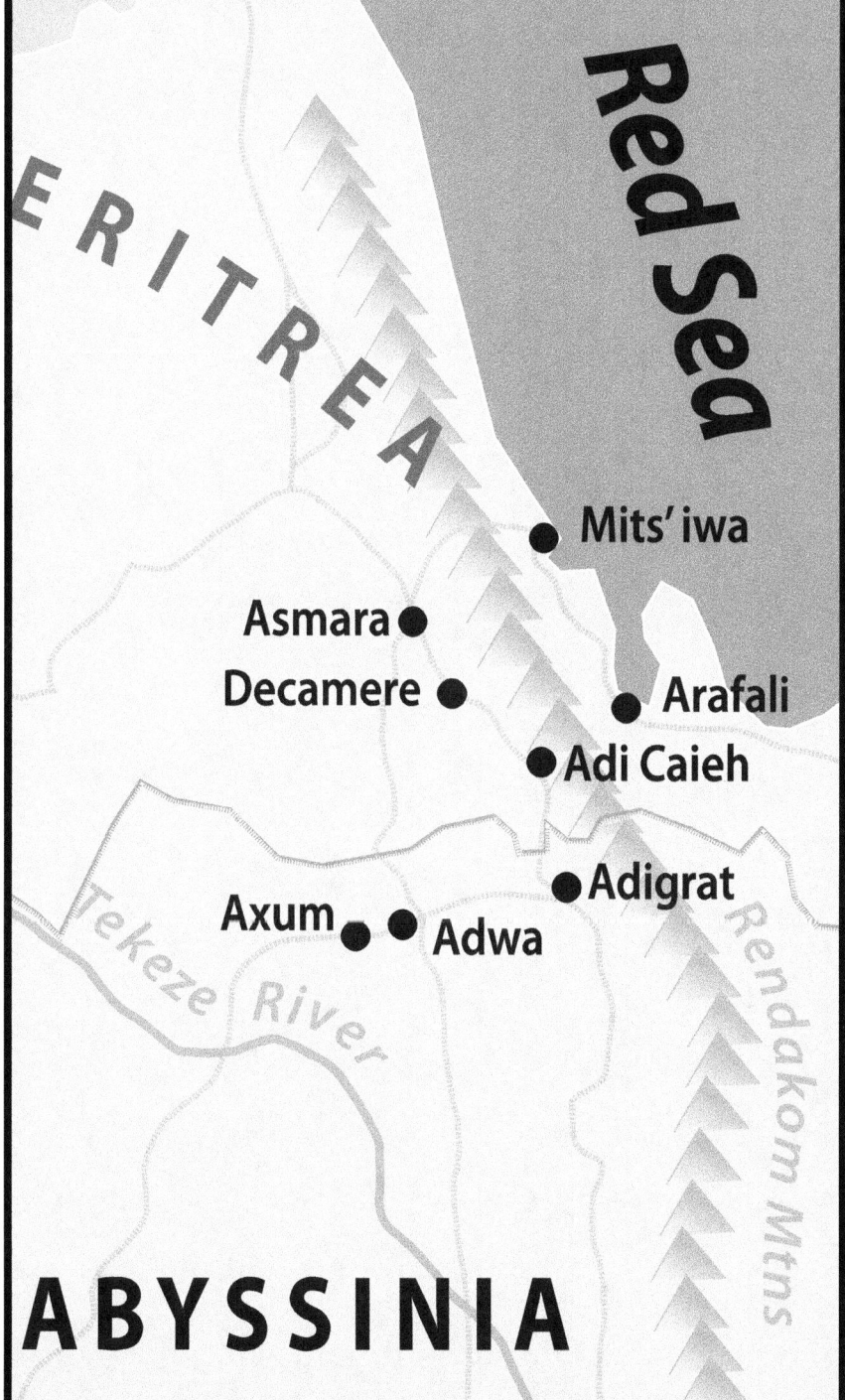

cast of characters

Prologue
- **Benito Mussolini** (1883 to 1945). The *Il Duce* fascist dictator of Italy from 1922 to 1943 and leader of the National Fascist Party
- **Haile Selassie** (1892 to 1975). Emperor of Abyssinia (Ethiopia) from 1930 to 1974, "The Lion of Judah;" rallied worldwide support for his resistance to the Italian invasion in 1935

Chapter 1
- **Sofia Savoy Russo, Ph.D.** Archeologist on a dig near Axum, Abyssinia
- **Ugo Sergreti.** Agent for the Organization for Vigilance and Repression of Anti-Fascism (OVRA)
- **Emanuel Boguchwal, Ph.D.** Chairman of Sofia's dissertation committee and close personal friend
- **King Victor Savoy Emmanuel III** (1869 to 1947). Regent of Italy during the fascists' regime.
- *Colonnello* **Adolfo Russo.** Sofia's deceased husband
- **Omar Mukhtar** (1862 to 1931). Arab guerilla leader in Italian-occupied Cyrenaica
- **Alonzo Russo.** Sofia's son
- *Counte Maggiore Generale* **Donato Savoy Russo.** Sofia's deceased father
- *Generale* **Rodolfo Graziani** (1883 to 1955). Viceroy of Italian East Africa and Marshal of the Italian Army in Abyssinia
- *Colonnello* **Jacopo Visco.** Head of the Italian secret police (OVRA) in the Axum area

Chapter 2

- **Walter James Gregory.** West Texas oilman, amateur archeologist, and part-time agent for the State Department's Bureau of Intelligence and Research
- **Mark William Gregory.** Walter's younger brother, seriously wounded while fighting in the Spanish Revolution
- **Hector Jonathan Ruiz.** Longtime employee of the Gregory Ranch and copilot of its Lockheed Electra Model 10
- **Elizabeth O'Toole Scalzitti.** Private-duty nurse hired to care for Mark Gregory
- *Generalissimo* **Francisco Franco** (1893 to 1975). Head of the Falange party and leader of the Nationalist Army in the Spanish Revolution
- **Sir Doctor Geoffrey St. John.** English volunteer surgeon for the Republican Army in the Spanish Revolution
- **Walter James Gregory.** Father of Walter and Mark, and patriarch of the Gregory ranch
- **Martha Alma (nee) Simpson Gregory.** Deceased wife of William and mother of Walter and Mark
- **President Sam Houston** (1793 to 1863). President of the Republic of Texas from 1836 to 1838 and 1841 to 1844
- **Colonel Theodore "Teddy" Roosevelt** (1858 to 1919). Leader of the Rough Riders in the Spanish-American War
- **General John "Black Jack" Pershing** (1860 to 1948). Leader of the American military expedition to capture the Mexican bandit Francisco "Pancho" Villa
- **Francisco "Pancho" Villa** (1878 to 1923). Mexican bandit and revolutionary who led his gang into Douglas, New Mexico, and murdered several American citizens

Chapter 3

- **Joseph Kabede.** Desk clerk at the Goha Hotel in Axum
- **Samia el Aslam, Phd.** Director of the African section of the Cairo Museum

Chapter 4

- **Doctor Oren Katsav, Ph.D.** Jewish archeologist from the British Mandate of Palestine and an expert in ancient languages
- **Doctor Malcolm Smyth Blackbourne, Ph.D.** Scientist at the Cairo Museum

- **Doctor Enrico Fermi, Ph.D.** (1901 to 1954). Nobel laureate, Professor of Physics at the University of Rome
- **Doctor Werner Heisenberg, Ph.D.** (1901 to 1976). Nobel laureate, nuclear physicist in Berlin
- **Minister Albert Speer** (1905 to 1961). The Nazis' Minister of Armaments
- **Admiral Wilhelm Canaris** (1887 to 1945). Head of the Nazi's Abwehr, German military intelligence
- **Sir Mycroft Terrance Howsham.** VC, OBE; British ambassador in Rome
- **Kendrew Rodric MacLeod.** Archeologist working a dig near Samarra in Iraq
- **Adam Smith.** American cultural attaché in Rome

Chapter 5
- **Silvestre Rodriquez, Ph.D.** Physicist on the scientific desk of the State Department's Bureau of Intelligence and Research
- **Doctor Forde Nørgaard, Ph.D.** Head of the State Department's Bureau of Intelligence and Research
- **Honorable Cordell Hull, Esq.** (1871 to 1955). Secretary of State from 1933 to 1944; Nobel Peace Prize laureate, 1945
- **President Franklin D. Roosevelt** (1882 to 1944). The 32nd President of the United States of America (1933 to 1944)
- **Doctor Max von Bloum, Ph.D.** Head of the president's Science Advisory Board
- **Harry Hopkins** (1890 to 1946). Roosevelt's chief diplomatic advisor and troubleshooter

Chapter 6
- *Onorevole* **Carlo Spada.** Italian ambassador to the United States of America
- *Onorevole* **Gian Galeazzo** (1903 to 1944). Minister of Foreign Affairs in Rome and Mussolini's son-in-law

Chapter 7
- **Tazio Di Pasqua.** King Emmanuel's personal secretary
- *Tenente* **Fiore Lazzari.** *Regia Aeronautica Italiana* aviator assigned to escort Sofia in Tobruk, Cyrenaica

Chapter 15
- **Aamir Sanawbar.** Eritrean fisherman and smuggler and skipper of a sambuk dhow

Chapter 16
- *Sergenta* **Egidio Santelli.** Rear gunner on the Savoia-Marchetti SM-84 scout plane
- *Capitano* **Danate Caito.** Commander of the OVRA's Alpine troops

Chapter 18
- **Kateb Fudial.** Proprietor of the general store in Mits'iwa
- **Shazeb Fudial.** Kateb's oldest son

Chapter 20
- *Capitano di Corvetta* **Nazario Tomaino.** Skipper of the Italian motor torpedo boat
- **Commander Harmon Deering, RN.** Senior MI6 agent in the British Crown Colony Aden

prologue

Hawzēr, near Axum, Abyssinia. 26 December 1935.

Tenente nente Ennio Angello leaned over the optical instrument and spoke clearly into the intercom, which was just an inch from his lips, "Right three degrees." The Tri-Motor Bomber Savoia-Marchetti SM-79 eased slightly to the right. Three seconds later, Angello said, "Right one degree." The roar of the three engines was deafening. "Steady." He paused. "Steady. Steady." He pushed the thumb button on a long cable. The Tri-Motor Bomber jumped a fraction upward.

Angello looked out the large Plexiglas window of the bomber's nose and observed the string of dozens of small canisters hurtling downward to the unarmed village below. In another second, he saw hundreds of other canister strings falling from the other five SM-79 bombers on this morning's raid.

Angello cracked a slow grin, and spoke into the microphone, "*Comandante, Capitano* Silvo Pala, on target. Look below."

Capitano Pala glanced out the side window and saw hundreds of canisters bursting inside the village. He shouted, "Good morning, Hawzēr. The *Regia Aeronautica Italiana* sends you our morning wakeup call."

chapter one

Axum, Abyssinia. Early May 1937.

At the end of her workday, archeologist and University of Rome professor Sofia Savoy Russo took short, deliberate strides on an indistinct trail along the Tekeze River—a tributary of the Blue Nile. Tall and willowy, with a lithe waist, she swung her arms in shallow arcs as her heavy, waterproof backpack bounced in rhythm with her pace. She needed time alone to ease her disquiet. The thirty-two-year-old tried to plan an exploration strategy for the next few days—her last on this dig.

She wore a tan bush jacket, khaki trousers, a light-green shirt, and short, tan cravat over her curved figure. Mid-calf, laced boots accentuated her long, shapely legs. Her long chestnut hair was pulled back into a bun and tucked under an Australian bush-style hat with chin strap. After a time, her angst eased and she absently began to hum and excerpt from *La Donna è Mobile*.

Sofia was a provocative beauty with a finely sculptured face, high cheekbones, wide, full mouth, luminous bistre-brown eyes, and nearly flawless bronze skin. Her gaze conveyed both empathy and a sparkle of youth. However, beneath her genteel façade was a hard sophistication, which was emphasized by her husky voice.

She was investigating several ancient burial sites for Abyssinian nobility in an area of exploration about twenty miles northeast of Axum. She felt thwarted because so far she had failed to find King Ezana's tomb. He was the sovereign who introduced Christianity to Abyssinia in the fourth century. She increased her pace as she deliberated on her predicament. She had only two days left to explore before her visa expired. Then, she and her two-man crew would have to drive to Axum in the four-wheel-drive Auto Union Explorer she had rented from her hotel. The following day, she would board a VIP CANT Z.1007 of the *Regia Aeronautica Italiana* for a flight to Khartoum, and from there continue her journey via Cairo on to Rome. She had left her camp alone on the pretext that she needed to heed "nature's call." Several minutes later, as she moved down the rough trail, she patted her Beretta thirty-two-caliber pistol in her jacket pocket. She had smuggled the pistol into Italian-occupied Abyssinia hidden in her surveyor's box. In the wilds of this sparsely explored territory, she knew it was best to be prepared for the unexpected.

Sofia was not only frustrated by the dig, she was also furious with her Italy-mandated guide, Ugo Segreti. Segreti was a fat, swarthy, shifty man with dark eyes, a moon face that was soft and flabby, and two fat chins, yet he moved with surprising agility. She suspected he was an agent for the *Organizzazione per la Vigilanza e la Repressione dell'Antifascismo*, or OVRA—the Italian secret police. Just the thought of him made her seethe with hot anger. He severely limited her movements, was irksome, and had dogged her repeatedly—always in her shadow. She also despised him because he frequently asked her impertinent questions, and all too frequently made lewd remarks.

A few days ago, while she had been bathing in a small stream, she had spotted Segreti looking at her through binoculars. With uncontrolled rage, she leaped out of the stream, ran up to him, knocked the binoculars away with her fist, and slapped him with all her might—knocking him to the ground. A large, red welt flamed on his cheek. She stood over him with her feet apart and her arms akimbo. A dark flame burned in her brown eyes and she shouted, "You *bastardo*, Segreti! If I ever see you spying on me again, I'll kill you. Do you understand me, *pervertito?*" After a few seconds, she calmed, and in a voice that was hardly more than a whisper, said "I'll kill you. I'll not tolerate any more of your spying on me. *Comprendere?*"

Segreti sat up, rubbed his swollen cheek, stared at Sofia with a cold, subdued fury in his hard, black eyes, and mumbled, "*Si, Signora.*"

Sofia had seen a grim, cynical smile twisting the corner of his mouth. She was confident Segreti would not report this incident to his OVRA handlers because of his own untoward conduct.

୧୨

Sofia loved her Italy, but hated the fascist government: their dictatorial policies, lawless thuggery, and barbaric treatment of minorities, especially the Jews. Her doctoral chairman, Doctor Emanuel Boguchwal, was a treasured mentor and a dear friend. Two years ago, Brown Shirt ruffians had arrested him without a charge and sent him to a concentration camp. No matter how hard she tried to discover his fate, the fascist bureaucracy rebuffed her.

Sofia was from a patrician family and was, in fact, the second cousin of the King of Italy, Victor Emmanuel Savoy III. She was a widow and had also lost her son.

After her husband's death, Sofia had become even more determined to continue her studies in archeology at the University of Sant'Anna Pisa, and she had earned her doctoral degree. She based her dissertation on her 1934 archeology dig near Axum, where she had searched for royal graves in Abyssinia with a special emphasis on the tomb of King Ezana.

Her mind wandered as she continued her walk. She thought about her deceased husband, *Colonnello* Adolfo Russo, who was killed in 1930 while supervising the construction of the hundred-mile, multi-layer, barbed-wire barrier extending from the Mediterranean port of Bardia some 270 kilometers south to the oasis Al-Jaghub. Omar Mukhtar, the Arab leader of the guerrillas fighting the Italian occupation of Cyrenaica, claimed credit for the kill.

She quickened her pace and tried to erase those painful memories. Instead, however, dreadful images of her son's murder in 1934 engulfed her. She gasped as the newsreel replayed in her mind of Black Shirt fascists parading down the Via Vittorio Veneto singing the praises of Benito Mussolini, *"Il Duce,"* fascist dictator of Italy, and waving black flags with fasces symbols. Alonzo was just seven years old. He and his chums from Saint Francis of Assisi School had thrown rocks at them? She had a feeling of pride that her son knew right from wrong even at such an early age and had taken action to express his disdain for the suppression he saw around him. The Black Shirts had stopped their parade and, in front of the spectators, clubbed Alonzo to death. His pals scattered and escaped.

Why now? Sofia asked herself. *Why is my mind filled now with such painful memories?* Her strides lengthened as she moved faster. *It's that damn Ugo Segreti who meddled with my mind.* She took several more strides. *Those terrible events were a long time ago and I've completed my grieving and am rebuilding my life.* She was unaware that her pace and stride were taking her far from her camp, down an uncharted path, and probably beyond the area she was authorized to explore. *I've got to continue on my new course.* She did not want her life defined by the deaths of her loved ones.

❧

The Italian government and military occupation forces had declared martial law in all of Italian East Africa—Abyssinia, Italian Somaliland, and Eritrea. The authorities restricted unauthorized persons from roaming around Abyssinia to prevent anyone from discovering evidence that the Italian military had used chemical and biological weapons for the mass killing of civilians in the just concluded war. If such evidence were found and presented to the League of Nations, it would be awkwardly embarrassing for the fascist government. It would prove that they had used such weapons in violation of the Geneva Protocol of 1928. The League might impose economic sanctions and diplomatic restrictions.

Sofia had gotten a visa to continue her research in Abyssinia only because of her kinship to the King, and because her father was an intimate friend of *Generale* Rudolfo Graziani, commander of the Italian troops in East Africa. As a special courtesy, Grazziani reluctantly endorsed Sofia's visa application for a short-term visit to continue her archeological research, and forwarded it to Rome for final approval. He added a warrant on Sofia's visa that restricted her movements to the archeological research area near Axum.

℘

Four weeks earlier:

Sofia strode to the desk to register in the Goha Hotel. An imposing, tall, dark man dressed in a black uniform with the fasces on his left shoulder and collar stepped in front of her. He stared at her with piercing-grey eyes that projected a cold light.

"*Signora* Russo, I am an OVRA agent." Without further introduction or explanation, he handed Sofia a white envelope with black trim and a large fasces in the center. "This summons commands you to report to the Organization for Vigilance and Repression of Anti-Fascism office tomorrow morning."

Sofia, alarmed at this sudden and aggressive intrusion by the Italian secret police, could barely gather her thoughts. She asked with confusion, "Why does the OVRA want me? I have a valid visa."

The agent turned to leave. "Be there."

℘

The following morning, there was a cool nip in Axum's seven-thousand-foot mountain air. The sun was low on the horizon, and the sky was a clear, deep blue—almost purple. Wildflowers covered open areas with a panoply of brilliant colors.

Sofia, dressed in her field ensemble, sat on a straight-back wooden chair in the dull-gray reception room of the OVRA office. Fearful of the unknown reason she had been summoned to the OVRA office, she fidgeted with her hair, crossed and uncrossed her legs at the ankles, and smoothed imaginary wrinkles in her trousers.

Eventually, a husky woman in the familiar black uniform entered and addressed Sofia. "Follow me."

Sofia rose and walked beside the woman down a long, dark-gray corridor. The woman opened the last door on the right and ordered Sofia, "Go in."

"Come into my office, *Signora* Russo, and sit down," commanded the man behind the desk.

Sofia, with fear grabbing her heart, entered as instructed. The dark-grey room was void of any decorations except for a large photograph of Benito Mussolini and a fascist flag. A single light bulb, cradled inside a dark shade, lighted the large room. She stood tense, poised, and slightly dazed. Near the back wall, a man dressed in the familiar black uniform sat behind the lone desk. "*Signora* Russo, come forward and you may sit," he offered.

"Thank you," Sofia spoke softly and crossed the room with slow deliberate steps, sitting in a chair that faced him.

He stared at her with shrewd, dark eyes set wide apart under a smooth, broad brow. "I am *Colonnello* Jacopo Visco, Head of OVRA in this area of Abyssinia." He was gaunt, swarthy, and vicious-looking, with a thin, hawk-like face. He was dressed in his tailored, black *Fascisti* uniform. The three, golden, five-pointed stars on his shoulder boards seemed to glow in the dim light. He adjusted his chair, leaned towards Sofia, and with a commanding voice said. "Your visa is valid for only four weeks. You must leave Abyssinia before it expires, otherwise, I will arrest you. Do you comprehend and agree to comply without reservation?"

She looked at him with fear widening in her eyes. "Yes, *Colonnello*," Sofia responded weakly.

"Very well." The *Colonnello* continued his intimidating stare at Sofia. "There are many hazards in this area. Accordingly, you must not wander outside of your exploration zone, which is about four square miles. I've outlined your zone on this map." He pushed the map across his desk towards Sofia. "When not working in this zone, you are to remain in or near your hotel. Is my directive clear, *Signora*?"

"Yes, sir." Sofia picked up the map, folded it, and put it in her coat pocket. "Your directive is perfectly clear and very restrictive. I'm not sure where the clues are that will direct my exploration. Please reconsider."

"*Signora*, my orders are firm. If you go outside of this area I will arrest you."

Sofia's face was taut and drained. Seething inside yet defeated, she agreed to the *Colonnello's* terms.

"Very well."

He leaned back in his chair, lit a cigarette, and a slow smirk crossed his face. "Your archeological site is fraught with hazards, such as unexploded ordnance and dangerous animals. To ensure you are protected in this acutely dangerous area, I have assigned a licensed guide, Mister Ugo Segreti, to accompany you whenever you are in the field on your dig. Additionally, Segreti will ensure your safety around the hotel, which is a hotbed of guerilla activity."

Shocked at this new and untoward restriction, she stood. "*Colonnello*, your restrictions are stifling and reduce significantly my chance for success. And I certainly don't need a nanny or a body-guard. You must take me for a fool." With conviction and in a firmer voice, she asserted, "I worked on a dig in this area for several months in 1934. I know it well. There is nothing to fear out there." She took a deep breath. "Keep your nanny," she declared. She started to leave, but stopped, sat back down, and said, "I'll protest to *Generale* Graziani, who is a close friend of my family."

Smiling with mockery, he responded, "Please do so, *Signora* Sofia Savoy Russo. Be certain to reference the General's memorandum of April first this year that details the warrants that I've just charged you to obey."

Intensely shocked, Sofia felt defeated. Tears trickled down her cheeks as she slumped into the chair. She could not look at *Colonnello* Visco and stared at the floor. She knew these fascists' bureaucratic roadblocks would almost guarantee failure of her dig.

Colonnello Visco continued in a softer voice. "Tomorrow morning, Mister Ugo Segreti will meet you at the hotel and follow you to the dig." He rose and with absolute conviction said, "I hope to see positive reports about your activities from Mister Segreti. Otherwise, I'll arrest you." He snubbed out his cigarette. "You may leave." With a wave of his hand he said, "Good luck on your dig."

ლ

Sofia reflected on that fateful morning and she realized that *Colonnello* Visco had not told her that Segreti was a mid-level agent of the Italian secret police. If perchance she did stumble upon artifacts from the war that the fascist government wanted to remain secret, she was certain that the Fascist government wanted to remain secret, she was convinced that Segreti's instructions were to ensure that she met with a fatal accident.

The trail narrowed as it became a path beside the steep bank of a small tributary of the Blue Nile. She spotted a small pile of rocks off the path configured as if it might have been a Christian cross. She moved off the path to inspect the sight to see if it might indicate a burial place. Focusing on the mound instead of her footing, she tripped over a partially buried rock, lost her balance, slipped, and slid about fifteen feet down the rocky and brush-covered bank's steep incline into the tributary. She had no serious injuries, but was bruised and scratched. Recovering from the shock of her fall, she started to swim to the bank. To her horror, she saw three crocodiles gliding swiftly towards her. To save herself, she allowed the cold, fast-moving water to push her over a short waterfall. She plummeted into a small pool about twenty feet below.

She surfaced in the icy cold water, took several deep breaths, and shook her head back and forth several times. She took a quick inventory and found that only her hat was missing. Her soaked clothes were unduly heavy but her waterproof backpack seemed intact, and she began to swim to shore. Her hat floated by and she grabbed it. She spotted a small opening in the side of the steep bank that was almost covered with brush and overgrowth.

Sofia's scientific curiosity compelled her to explore it. The opening was just large enough to admit small animals. She chipped at the rubble with her rock axe and, in a few minutes, the opening was large enough for her to enter.

She crawled in the narrow opening and flicked on her flashlight. When she entered, the air was musty. She scanned the light over the floor and sides of the cave but could not see the end. Inside, the cave was tall enough for her to stand comfortably. Within a few steps, she heard the telltale hiss of a puff adder—a dangerous reptile that had caused more death in Africa than any other snake. She spotted the reptile several feet away, coiled against the opposite wall. She gasped and small beads of perspiration formed on her forehead. Undaunted, she drew her Beretta 32, aimed at the reptile, and emptied the magazine at it. The loud gunshots echoed back and forth between the cave's walls, causing a chaotic din that sent sharp, stabbing pain into her ears. The reptile died in pieces.

It took several seconds for Sofia to gather her composure. Cautiously, she proceeded deeper into the cave, watchful for hazards. About a hundred feet farther, she saw several terra cotta amphorae scattered along the floor. She stooped to examine them. Their stoppers were made of clay and sealed with pitch. Several were broken, reveal a collection of parchments, some of which were in small fragments. She recognized the amphorae as very old, and understood, with minimal investigation, that she had probably just made an important archeological find.

The fragments were very fragile. She withdrew her field notebook from her backpack along with a spade. She carefully lifted a few fragments and put them between pages in her notebook. Then she spotted one of the parchments that was almost whole, and saw that it was inscribed in an ancient language she could not recognize. She examined the remaining broken amphorae, but only two more contained documents. As she prepared to leave, she put several amphorae shards into the side pockets of her bush jacket. She crawled out and shoved rocks and shrubbery across the opening to conceal it.

It was almost dark when Sofia returned to camp. She was worried that Ugo Segreti had left camp to report her missing. Fortunately, his vehicle was parked next to his tent. When her porter pointed to Segreti's tent and nodded his head, she knew that Segreti was inside. Summoning all her courage to face him, she snapped open the tent flap, entered, and found him passed out, with an empty bottle of grappa on the ground. She sighed deeply and began to relax as her adrenaline subsided. *The* idiota *probably didn't even know that I'd left camp*

Alone in her tent, Sofia withdrew the notebook and placed a few of the parchment fragments on her small tent table. A single kerosene lantern lit her tent. She examined the fragments with her magnifying glass, saw a Christian cross, and concluded that the script might be some form of Amharic. Her heart skipped a beat as she wondered if this collection contained the clues she needed to find King Ezana's burial site.

Sofia decided not to reveal what she had found until she had more information. She knew there were unscrupulous grave looters who would defile the site and sell the artifacts for a few coins. She was sorely disappointed that her time in Abyssinia was almost over and she did not have time to explore the cave further. Her consolation was that she would seek expert consultants to help her decipher and understand what she had found.

chapter two

Gregory Ranch, near Odessa, Texas. 7 May 1937.

The deafening roar of the twin Pratt & Whitney Wasp engines flooded the cockpit of the Lockheed Model 10 Electra.

Walter Gregory had departed Norfolk, Virginia, about ten hours earlier, which included a short refueling stop in Memphis. He had another hour to touchdown at Sloan Airport, the twin-city airfield centered between Odessa and Midland, Texas. At thirty-nine years of age, the six-foot, 195-pound, sandy-haired Texan had spent years in the oil fields of West Texas and was no stranger to facing challenges head on.

A crosswind had caused the Lockheed Electra to veer off course slightly. Walter adjusted his heading two degrees right to maintain his course. The petrol gauge indicated that the main petrol tank was one-quarter full. He switched to an auxiliary petrol tank and noticed the Electra was slightly nose-heavy. He rotated the trim wheel a fraction and the aircraft was in trim and on course.

❧

Walter had charted a Pan American Sikorsky Flying Boat, model VS-44 to fly his younger brother, Mark William Gregory from Barcelona to Norfolk. Mark, a member of the Abraham Lincoln Brigade, had been seriously wounded in the Spanish Civil War.

Walter had the plane's passenger cabin configured to accommodate the hospital bed and related medical equipment for his wounded brother. He hired the private-duty nurse Elizabeth Scalzitti to care for Mark on their trans-Atlantic flight and then on the Electra to their hometown of Odessa.

An ambulance was standing by at Sloan Airport to take Mark, Walter, and Elizabeth to the Regency Hospital in Odessa. Hector Ruiz was Walter's copilot, a longtime employee of the Gregory family, and his close friend. Hector would pilot the Electra to the private landing strip on the Gregory ranch near Penwell, about 20 miles southwest in Ector County.

ა

Walter spoke to Hector through his throat microphone on the aircraft's intercom system. "Hector, you've got the controls. I'm going aft to check on Mark. It's probably time for his morphine shot."

Mark was a young idealist, and during his senior year at Dartmouth University, he had joined the Socialist Party of America. Believing in the righteousness of Marxism, he volunteered to fight General Francisco Franco's fascist revolution in Republican Spain. He was in no man's land charging a Moraccan trench when a German 88 shell exploded behind him and sent shrapnel tearing into his legs and lower back.

To save Mark's life, Sir Geoffrey St. John, an English volunteer surgeon for the Republican Army, had to amputate both of Mark's legs above the knees.

Walter took a long look at his sleeping brother and checked the straps holding Mark to the hospital bed. "How's he doing?" he asked Elizabeth.

Elizabeth responded, "He's been asleep for over an hour. His vital signs are normal, and his breathing is slightly shallow, probably due to the opiates."

"Very well. Let's check those bandages."

He carefully removed the sheet and blanket that covered Mark. Walter and Elizabeth carefully inspected the bandages over the stumps for stains. "None. He's doing as well as we can expect." She pulled the sheet and blanket over Mark, "This trip is telling on him. We need to get him to Regency Hospital as soon as possible."

"We're about an hour out."

The hubbub awoke Mark and he looked up at Walter and the nurse through hazy eyes. He pointed a clumsy index finger at the nurse and mumbled, "Who are you?"

Walter took his hand. "Hi, Mark. Welcome to the real world. How are you feeling?"

Mark looked at Walter, "OK, I reckon. I'm a mess, am I not?" He took a long pause and tried to regain control of his emotions. "Thanks for taking care of me."

"That's what big brothers are for. We're due for touchdown at Sloan in about fifty minutes. Dad has an ambulance waiting to take us to the Regency Hospital in Odessa."

Mark gave a quick nod. He knew his condition was serious, as Walter's usual sly good humor and ready smile had been replaced by a somber countenance.

"I ought to check Mark's vital signs before we land," Elizabeth said.

Walter nodded and continued holding Mark's hand as Elizabeth completed her tasks. Elizabeth smiled broadly at Mark. "Good news, your vital signs are normal. Are you ready for your morphine shot?"

Mark blinked twice.

Walter raised Mark's arm and Elizabeth administered the narcotics. "I'll awaken you after touchdown in Odessa."

❧

Walter joined his father, Wallis James Gregory, on the front porch and stared into the setting sun. He watched several whitetail deer grazing nearby. "Why are you standing there like a dead tree?" Wallis growled. "Sit down, son, and have a shot of this sour mash with me—it's freshly distilled."

Walter complied. He knew his father's bark was worse than his bite. And he had to admit that his father had mellowed some since becoming a widower. Martha Alma (nee Simpson) Gregory, Walter's mother and Wallis's wife, had died of influenza in 1920.

Walter stared at the vast expanse of the Gregory spread—over 120,000 acres, as far as the eye could see in any direction. He smiled inwardly with pride as he reminisced on the history of this ranch and its hundred-year-old Gregory brand, *WJG*.

President Sam Houston had deeded this land grant to Walter's great-grandfather, Walter, in 1837 for his heroic actions in the Battle of San Jacinto. The land deed had been passed down to firstborn males in the Gregory family ever since. Wallis, continuing his family's tradition of service to their country, charged San Juan Hill with Colonel "Teddy" Roosevelt and his Rough Riders in 1898. A Spanish bullet in his left leg left him partially crippled, requiring him to use a cane when he walked.

In 1929, wildcatters discovered high-grade oil on the Gregory ranch near Penwell, a tiny farming community encircled by the Gregory ranch. Wallis signed an oil lease for $500,000 with the Permian Basin Oil Company for 45,000 acres near Penwell. Overnight, the Gregory family became one of the richest families in West Texas. Over the next few years, the ever-increasing royalty dollars had made the Gregory family millionaires many times over.

Wallis remarked, "Thanks for bringing Mark home and taking care of him. Reckon he'll do all right in that hospital with that nurse taking charge. She's a real gem. Where did you find her?"

"Elizabeth is the sister of one of my classmates from Tech and is a well-regarded private-duty nurse from Houston. It was just a matter of a telephone call to hire her. You're right; she looks after Mark as if he were her own brother."

Wallis asked, "Well and good, but what the hell are we going to do to help Mark overcome his depression and get him fit enough to help me run our business? Now that you got your own outfit to run, Mark is our only viable option."

Walter nodded silently.

Wallis took a deep drink of the sour mash. "I don't blame you. It's what you ought to do. But you need a wife to settle down and raise a family."

Walter took a sip, put his glass on the bamboo side table and replied, "Indeed, Dad, I've got to ease out of the family business and pay more attention to my activities. Mark is the man to take my place."

In 1916, Walter had joined General John Pershing's expeditionary force to find the Mexican revolutionary Francisco "Pancho" Villa in retaliation for Villa's raid and slaughter of American citizens in Columbus, New Mexico.

Later, he graduated from Texas Tech University with a major in petroleum engineering and a minor in business management. For several years, he had been his father's right-hand man in the management of their vast empire of cattle ranching and oil production. He garnered a reputation as a savvy businessman who was honest, fair, and aggressive, but not ruthless.

A few years after graduation, Walter had formed the Permian Geophysical and Production Company. He traveled worldwide searching for oil deposits in the East Indies, China, South America, the Middle East, and Africa. In only a few years, he became a multimillionaire in his own right. He used his Leica 35mm camera to document his geophysical and petroleum-drilling activities, and relevant scenes and officials of his host country.

During his travels, Walter became interested in archeology. In 1933 he traveled to Abyssinia, the center of the Axum Empire, to search for ancient royal graves and to uncover burial artifacts. He found some tantalizing clues pertaining to the burial site of King Ezana but, to his dismay, he did not find the tomb.

Walter had a strong love for his country and served as an informal international agent for the State Department's Bureau of Intelligence and Research. His profession as a petroleum engineer and his amateur archeology provided an excellent cover. On return from an overseas trip, Walter would stop in Washington, D.C., to brief the Bureau's intelligence personnel. Topics included profiles of government officials, commercial activities, foreign influences, military capabilities and intentions, and human rights violations. He brought captioned photographic prints to augment his briefings. After his third trip to the State Department, they had granted him a Secret clearance.

Walter continued, "We'll have to send Mark to a psychiatrist for extensive therapy."

Wallis cocked his head and with intense eyes stared at Walter. "Those idiot shrinks are no damn good for nothin'. What that boy needs is hard work and good West Texas air." He took a deep drink. "He needs the same clean air that helped heal my left leg when I returned from Cuba in 'ninety-eight." Wallis tapped his cane several times on the wood floor and said, "I still hate those damn Spaniards. I hate those damn Communist Spaniards more. My boy would still have his legs if he was not seduced by their treacherous agitprop."

"Dad, you mean prosthetic legs."

"I don't care what you call it. We're gonna make Mark whole again."

Walter responded, "That's our only option."

"So it is. We'll do OK. Josh sure knows how to distill that corn."

Walter relaxed, took a sip, and began to discuss what he had seen in Spain, and his awareness that Germany and Italy were preparing for another world war.

Wallis cocked his head and focused intently on Walter. "You reckon that's the way it is?"

"Dad, I've no doubt. The fascists are exercising their war plans in Spain, and the Germans are bristling to toss off the harsh terms of the Versailles Treaty."

"Then we need to get Mark back to work as soon as possible. When that war starts, the U S of A is gonna need oil, one hell of a lot of oil. And we'll supply 'em with West Texas light, the best oil there is! Get your geophysical crews all over West Texas to find more likely deposits. We'll drill exploratory wells, and we'll punch 'em down deep to get that oil. If the refineries can't process all that oil, we'll build our own."

A servant came out and asked, "Mister Gregory, can I get you anything?"

"No, thanks, Lucia. We're fine. You go ahead and turn in. We're just gonna stay out here for a piece, work on this sipping whiskey, and talk a spell."

chapter three

Cairo Museum, Egypt. 10 May 1937.

ofia's visa would expire in two days. She dismissed her two-man crew, packed her equipment, and went to the OVRA office to get her airplane ticket. Later, in her room at the hotel, she reflected on the meeting with despair.

Colonnello Visco with formal aplomb had stamped her passport and issued her an export visa. "I have reserved a seat for you on our *Regia Aeronautica Italiana* flight for Cairo tomorrow. Its scheduled departure is 0800 hours. There will be a two-hour refueling stop in Khartoum. It is to your advantage to be on this airplane; if you are not, I will arrest you."

He then withdrew a dark cigarette from his case and with an exaggerated flourish lit it. "*Signora*, you will find this airplane quite comfortable. It is a model CANT Z.1007 Tri-Motor Bomber modified as a VIP transport aircraft." She bristled at his mocking voice when he commented, "Have a pleasant trip, *Signora*."

Exhausted and frustrated, Sofia walked into the lobby of the Goha Hotel and told the desk clerk, Joseph Kabede, that she would be checking out tomorrow. She returned the keys to the Explorer, paid her bill, and arranged transport to the airport.

"We're sorry you have to leave. You've been an excellent guest." Joseph stumbled a bit and fiddled with her keys. "May I offer the complimentary use of our bar and restaurant for the evening as a small token of our esteem?"

"That's very kind and I accept with pleasure. I need a serious boost. Please have the clerk take my equipment to my room."

Sofia selected a table in the corner, leaned back in the chair, and ordered a bottle of Cappellano Rupestris.

"*Si, Signora*," the waiter responded with a large smile. "We had one case of this fine wine, and now only a few bottles remain." He scanned the room and said, "We have such a fine wine for our important, very important Italian officers. We do our best to honor their majestic presence in our poor country."

After her first glass of wine, Sofia began to relax and the frustration of the dig began to fade. Soon, she heard the voice from hell. "Good evening, *Signora* Russo. I will join you on your last day to drink a toast to our association." Ugo Segreti spoke with a faint mocking tone. Without waiting for an answer, he sat in a chair opposite Sofia, and signaled the waiter for another glass.

Sofia stared at Segreti with icy eyes, viewing him as a carrier of pestilence. "I don't have any business with you, Segreti. I'm leaving tomorrow. Leave me alone!"

Segreti filled his glass, drank heartily, and said, with a harsh edge to his voice, "You are my charge, *Signora* Russo, and I will be with you until you board that airplane tomorrow morning. *Comprendere?*"

As her ire rose, Sofia cracked a small smile void of mirth, rose purposefully, and tossed her glass of wine in his face. "Enjoy my wine." She picked up the wine bottle and marched out of the bar to the stairs and on to her room.

☙

Sofia's ten-hour flight to Cairo was uneventful. She worked on the report of her dig, leaving out her discovery of the amphora and shards, and her contretemps with Segreti. Once in Rome she would polish it into a formal paper and submit it to a peer review committee for publication in *Documenta Praehistorica*.

As Sofia stepped off the CANT at the Cairo airport late that afternoon, the intense heat and heavy humidity caused her to gasp. The long walk to the terminal sapped what energy she had remaining. Inside the terminal, she headed for the bar, ordered a bottle of chilled soda, and gulped it down. Refreshed, she claimed her baggage, ordered a taxicab to take her to the Shepheard Hotel, checked into her suite, stripped, showered in the cool water, and crawled into the sumptuous bed. For the first time in weeks, she was totally relaxed and slept deeply.

⌘

Cairo Museum, Egypt. 17 May 1937.

"Good morning, my dear Sofia," Doctor Samira el Aslam said. "How wonderful to see you after all these years." He smiled broadly. "You are more beautiful than ever." Samira was a small and slender person with thin features and a quick manner. However, his deep, black eyes projected a powerful man of great intellect.

Sofia, in a bright-blue frock and a chic matching chapeau, took his hands and kissed him on both cheeks. "My dear friend, I've missed you." Her strong, radiant face shone without makeup.

"Tell me, what has happened? Last I heard, you were on a dig in Abyssinia. What brings you to Cairo? You have something for me?"

Doctor Samira was a member of Sofia's dissertation committee, and the director of the African section of the Cairo Museum. He was a renowned expert on ancient funeral rites.

"Let's go to my office, relax, and sip cool green tea; it refreshes the soul on these horribly stuffy days."

Artifacts of all stripes cluttered Samira's office. He removed books and papers from a chair for Sofia.

Sofia recounted her adventures in Abyssinia and the clues she'd discovered regarding King Ezana's tomb. With a firm voice she said,

"I'm close to finding it. I know it." She sipped her tea and smoothed an imaginary crease in her dress. "I need more time at the site. But those idiot OVRA fascists forced me to leave. Why they are afraid of me is beyond my comprehension. I had nothing to do with their obscene war in Abyssinia."

"Unfortunate. Indeed, unfortunate. Will the authorities allow you to return?"

"Perhaps. I don't know. Those fascists are paranoid and unpredictable. I'll try. Maybe I'll ask my cousin for help."

"King Victor Emmanuel Savoy?" Samira leaned forward and with a puzzled look said, "Be cautious, my dear Sofia. He is a puppet king to Mussolini's Black Shirts and remains king only as long as he does the fascists' bidding."

Sofia dismissed Samira's last comment with a brief, "We'll see." She opened her briefcase and withdrew two shards and a few of the parchment fragments. "Here are some of the items I found in a cave near Axum." She laid them on Doctor Samira's desk and related the adventure that led her to find these artifacts. "What do you make of them?"

Samira picked up one of the shards and inspected it carefully. He used his ten-power loupe to examine some strange markings. "These shards are very old and are some sort of terra cotta. I'll run a few tests to determine their composition. It's these markings that piqued my interest. I don't know what they are, but at first glance, the text appears to be in ancient Aramaic."

"That makes sense," said Sofia, "The language in Abyssinia is a derivative of Aramaic."

"I'll work on it." Samira put the shards aside. "Let's see what these parchments tell us." Using flat-based tweezers, he picked up one of the parchment fragments and placed it on a blackened glass slide. After a few moments of inspection through the microscope, he looked up and said, "A mystery." He examined the remaining parchments. "These images have faded appreciably and appear to be some form of ancient Aramaic. These marks could be part of a drawing—a female, it appears." He looked at Sofia. "My deductions are tentative. I have only a cursory knowledge of Aramaic." He placed the glass slide on his desk. "May I keep these fragments?"

"Yes. Of course. Do what you can. I'll contact you in a few weeks."

"I'll ask a colleague for his help. His specialty is ancient languages." He leaned back in his chair. "My dear Sofia, you bring me this intriguing puzzle to distract me." He patted her hands as a large smile enveloped his face. "It's been far too long since we've seen each other. Have a glass of wine with me, and let's talk about 'sealing wax, cabbages and kings.'"

❧

Two days later, Sofia boarded the local train for Alexandria. Six hours after that, she checked into the Le Metropole Hotel. The next morning she boarded an Italian train and the conductor escorted her to a bedroom compartment for the twenty-six-hour trip to Tripoli in Italian Cyrenaica.

At the Cyrenaica border checkpoint, a tall, raw-boned, hard-faced, and strongly built OVRA agent with a rough-edged voice quizzed Sofia extensively about her stay in Egypt. "Do you have any illegal contraband? What were you doing at the Cairo Museum? Whom did you see? What did you discuss?" He continued with dozens of other personal questions.

Sofia snapped at the fellow, "Why should I answer your questions? Obviously, you already know the answers. Your agents have followed me since I arrived in Egypt."

"You'll answer because the OVRA asks them."

"Stop this nonsense. You're harassing me." With her anger rising she spouted, "I am an Italian citizen traveling on an Italian passport with the proper OVRA visas. Get out of my compartment."

The agent did not yield and demanded, "*Signora* Sofia Savoy Russo, it is not your right to question or order the OVRA. Either cooperate or I will arrest you." With a punishing fury, he pulled her luggage out of the closet and ransacked the suitcases, throwing her clothing and personal items helter-skelter about her compartment.

With a choke in her voice, she said, "What do you want of me?"

With a thin, insincere smile, he quipped, "Nothing, *Signora* Russo. You may pass."

Fortunately, the fellow had not searched her equipment boxes, which meant that her Beretta 32 was safe.

The next day she boarded the *S. S. Rex, Italia* bound for Naples.

chapter four

Cairo Museum, Egypt. 2 June 1937.

octor Samira sent a letter to his colleague Doctor Oren Katsav, a respected Jewish archeologist from the British Mandate of Palestine, a man skilled in ancient languages. Samira outlined the background of the parchments he enclosed, and asked Katsav if he would inspect them and reply with his findings.

While waiting for a response from Doctor Katsav, Samira photographed the shards with a 4x5 Graflex camera. He exposed the two sheets of film in a film holder, placed the holder on a table, and inadvertently placed one of the shards atop the holder. He obtained a fresh film holder and continued his work. When he developed the exposed film the next day, he saw the outline of the shard on one of the negatives. Physical science was not his forte, but he knew that the shard had to be radioactive to leave its image on the negative. He contacted his science colleague at the museum, Doctor Malcolm Smyth-Blackbourne, and asked to borrow his Geiger counter to scan the shard.

A Geiger counter's scale is calibrated in a number of radiation counts per minute and is color-coded: low levels of radiation are noted on the green end of the scale, moderate levels are in yellow, and the higher counts are in red. He saw the scale's needle oscillating slightly between the yellow and red counts per minute, which puzzled him. *How much radiation is normal? And how much over normal is the radiation on the shards?* Determined to solve this radioactive mystery, he sent a cablegram to his old friend Doctor Enrico Fermi, a theoretical physicist at the University of Rome. Samira detailed his findings and asked Fermi if he would study the shard's radioactivity and report his findings. He concluded his cablegram by saying the shard was loaned to him by an Italian archeologist working near Axum in Abyssinia.

In a cablegram the following day, Doctor Fermi asked Samira to send a sample of the shards.

I'LL WORK ON THIS INVESTIGATION AS SOON AS I RECEIVE YOUR SAMPLES STOP I WILL REPORT MY FINDINGS VIA CABLEGRAM STOP

Several days after receiving the shards, Fermi completed his research and concluded that the dust's radioactivity was about thirty-five percent higher than normal. He concluded that the radiation was probably due to several uranium isotopes. Unfortunately, he did not have the engineering expertise or the equipment to quantify his findings.

Meanwhile, Doctor Katsav had concluded that the inscriptions on the parchments were an early version of Amharic that was used in ancient Jerusalem. He surmised that the faded drawing on one parchment was of a female with a large bust and Negroid features. He suspected that the writings on the fragments pertained to the Queen of Sheba, her treasure, and her burial. But without more fragments, he could not make a firm conclusion. He sent his findings to Samira and said, "Should you find more of these parchments, please send them to me. Perhaps we can solve one of the enduring mysteries of Jewish history in Abyssinia."

∽

Fermi's professional pride was piqued by the incomplete assessment of the radioactive dust on the shards. Resigned, he contacted Doctor

Werner Heisenberg in Berlin. Heisenberg was a Nobel laureate for his work in theoretical nuclear physics and was Fermi's old friend and professional associate. Fermi knew that Heisenberg was working on the nature of atoms, and that he was conducting engineering research with uranium-235, trying to develop a controllable and sustainable nuclear chain reaction—nuclear fission.

Fermi, a silent anti-fascist, knew Heisenberg was working for Albert Speer, the Nazi Minister of Armaments, and was financed by Admiral Wilhelm Canaris of the Abwehr, German Military Intelligence. Fermi was almost certain that Heisenberg was not cooperating fully with Speer. At a scientific conference in Lucerne the year before, during private meetings, Heisenberg had hinted vaguely that he had deliberately sabotaged his own research to prevent any usable nuclear information on the production of an atomic bomb from getting to the Nazis. Accordingly, Fermi tasked one of his post-doctoral associates to deliver one shard to Heisenberg. But, just to make sure, he did not relate the background of these shard fragments.

In an airmail letter, two weeks later, Heisenberg confirmed that the dust on the shard was suffused with various isotopes of high-grade uranium ore, and was abnormally rich in uranium-235. He wrote, "One should be cautious in handling it. Keep the shard in a safe and use tongs to hold it. Caution all who touch it." Out of professional curiosity, Heisenberg also asked where the shard had been unearthed.

Fermi knew with near certainty that within a few years there would be a world war, one pitting the aggressive Italian fascists and the ignoble German Nazis against the Western democracies. Accordingly, he was disinclined to share any information about the source of the shard. He responded with the lie that an old friend in Persia had sent the shard to him, and that he knew nothing else about it.

Understanding the importance of Heisenberg's information concerning uranium-235—the essential element needed for the theoretical atomic bomb. Fermi decided that he must share this critical information with a democratic government, possibly the United States of America.

Fermi sent a message to Doctor Samira saying that he could not determine the exact nature of the radioactivity, but nonetheless to use precautions when handling it.

Fermi, now seriously concerned that he was on the cusp of an important scientific discovery with serious political implications, called the United States Embassy and asked for the cultural attaché.

"That will be Mister Adam Smith. Just a moment, I'll connect you," responded the telephone switchboard operator.

While waiting for the connection, Fermi envisioned that the damnable OVRA was monitoring all telephone calls to the Embassy.

"Good morning, Doctor Fermi. Your reputation precedes you. How may I be of service?" Smith said in his most professional voice.

"I should like to meet with you to ask your opinion regarding a slight matter of some cultural curiosity—if you would have interest."

Smith's keen senses went on full alert. A Nobel laureate of Doctor Enrico Fermi's reputation typically did not want to discuss "small" matters. Smith was a slim, wiry fellow with thinning, brownish-grey hair and intelligent blue eyes behind thick, black-rimmed glasses. His out-ward persona belied the fact that he was a senior agent with the State Department's Bureau of Intelligence and Research. He had earned his Master of Science degree in physics from St. Mary's University in San Antonio. "Of course, Doctor Fermi, I'd be delighted to meet you." He flipped through a stack of papers on his desk. "The ambassador is hosting a reception this evening for some visiting congressmen. Would it be convenient for you to attend?"

"Yes, of course. The particulars?"

"Eight o'clock and black tie. I'll send a messenger 'round with an invitation. Your address and telephone number, please." He noted the information and returned the receiver to its cradle. His mind whirled. *What's on Fermi's mind?* After a few minutes of fruitless speculation, he drafted a Top Secret message to the State Department alerting them to the pending visit and asking if they had any operations pending that might include Doctor Fermi.

Within two hours, Smith received a response from the Secretary. "Befriend Doctor Fermi. Send all information directly to me. Priority."

The reception was a gala affair. The full orchestra played a potpourri of waltzes, jazz tunes, and the latest songs from Tin Pan Alley. Ladies were dressed in beautiful gowns and festooned with sparkling jewelry. And fine French champagne flowed freely. Smith recognized Fermi from his photographs and towards mid-evening introduced himself to the doctor. After a few minutes of small talk, Smith suggested that they move to the terrace so they might talk in private.

"You are aware of my work in theoretical nuclear physics, I assume?"

"Of course, Doctor Fermi. You are well-known throughout the scientific community. Your papers are required reading in the graduate physics departments in many of our universities." The pair continued walking and arrived at the deserted terrace.

"Doctor Fermi, I am a representative of the United States Government, and I must ask why you've requested this private meeting. What is on your mind?"

Fermi seemed slightly nervous, and he looked around to reassure himself that they were alone. He stated, with a tinge of emotion, "I have several pottery shards, and the dust on them has an extraordinary amount of radioactivity that is especially rich in uranium-235, and other unstable isotopes are present."

Fermi moved to the other side of Smith and checked the door to the terrace. "I did not have the expertise or equipment to make an exact analysis of these uranium isotopes. Accordingly, I sent one shard to my friend, Doctor Werner Heisenberg, in Berlin, for his analysis."

Smith was intrigued and, with his science background, he understood the implications of this radioactive shard in German hands. He responded with disquiet, "Heisenberg? He's working for Albert Speer and the Abwehr."

Before Smith could continue, Fermi interrupted, "I understand your concern. Please realize that I am with you in our political beliefs. However, I make no point of broadcasting it. I am confident that Heisenberg is also with us. Last year at a conference he hinted broadly that he deliberately sabotaged his research when trying to develop a controlled and sustainable nuclear reaction."

"That had better be the case," Smith cracked. "We've got to put a clamp on this information all 'round. This is momentous intelligence that the Nazis would kill for." Smith looked over the terrace rail at the garden. "How did you come by this radioactive shard? I need to know about anyone who has this information."

"As far as I know, two other people are involved. Doctor Samira el Aslam, my friend who is the curator of the African section at the Cairo Museum, discovered that the shards were radioactive and sent them to me for scientific evaluation." Fermi paused to confirm that he had the remaining sequence of events correct. "I understand that Doctor Samira got the shards from an Italian female archeologist. She found them somewhere near Axum while on a dig for Abyssinian royal tombs."

"What's her name, and how can I contact her?" Smith demanded.

"I do not know the name of the archeologist or anything about her. I'll cable Samira tomorrow for details."

"What are Doctor Samira's politics?

"As far as I know, Samira has no politics. His world is archeology."

"You'd best ask him to keep mum about the shards, but don't go into detail about why. Just tell him that the shards are involved in some legal proceedings. Call me to arrange a meeting as soon as you get the information. We have to act quickly. We don't want to compete with the fascists for Uranium ore."

☙

Two days later, Fermi was in Smith's office. "Were you followed, Doctor?"

"I doubt it. I took a roundabout way and changed taxicabs several times."

"Okay. What do you have?"

"The female archeologist is Doctor Sofia Savoy Russo, a professor at the University of Rome." He relayed what other few details he'd discovered about her.

"Anything else, Doctor Fermi?"

"Nothing."

"Thank you for your help. I'll contact you in a few days with an update. Let me know if I may be of help now or anytime in the future." Smith shook Fermi's hand and said, "Use the mail to keep in touch with me. Goodbye."

That afternoon, Smith energized his intelligence net to build a comprehensive dossier on Doctor Russo. Within a few days he had details about her which included her family background and her familial relationship with King Savoy, the death of her husband and son, her education, character, proclivities, vices, and professional career in education and archeology. Her politics he surmised to be quietly anti-fascist. And he had a copy of her preliminary report on her latest dig in Abyssinia.

He drafted a cablegram for the Navy's message/cryptographic center to send to the State Department in which he relayed the dossier on Doctor Sofia Savoy Russo and more information about the radioactive shards. Because of its time-sensitive intelligence, Smith had the communication operators tag it IMMEDIATE, classify it Top Secret, code word KAPPA, and address it to the Bureau of Intelligence and Research.

chapter five

The White House, Washington, D.C. 10 August 1937.

for several weeks, Adam Smith's top-secret code-word message was shuffled among several desks at the State Department's Bureau of Intelligence and Research. Staffers did not recognize its importance and were not interested in doing the research to understand its implications. They were disdainful of following mandated security procedures for such a highly classified document. Several days later, the office messenger on her morning rounds cavalierly dropped Smith's message into the "In" basket of Silvestre Rodriquez—an integral member of the Scientific section.

Rodriquez had earned his doctorate in nuclear physics from the University of Texas several years before and his committee recognized his intelligence and energetic work ethic. The co-eds, however, noticed his tall, lanky physique, jet-black, wavy hair, and piercing, green eyes. Later that morning, he emptied his "In" basket and scanned the pile: circulars, management's general memos, announcements, and various unsolicited, unimportant pieces of correspondence. "What junk," he mumbled, as he went through the stack. Eventually, he picked up Adam Smith's message, and saw the code-word intelligence classification.

The subject line piqued his curiosity. He read the first few lines and stopped cold. He hunched over his desk, adjusted his glasses, and moved his desk lamp closer. He read the entire message, reviewed the two concluding paragraphs, leaned back in his chair, and worked to recall the details of class #526, Advanced Theory of Atomic Physics. Snippets of Fermi's and Heisenberg's papers on nuclear fission raced through his mind. Quantum theory suggested that a tremendous amount of energy would be released by the nuclear fission of U-235 in a controlled nuclear chain reaction. He scooted his chair closer to his desk and slowly reread the message, absorbing every word. His mind raced, and he made margin comments in scientific notation. After a few minutes, he deduced the full import of the information in Smith's message.

His heart rate increased and small beads of perspiration formed on his brow. He whispered under his breath, "My God!" With careful precision, he slipped the message into a top-secret envelope, and placed it in his portfolio.

With long, purposeful strides, he reached the office of Doctor Forde Nørgaard, the head of the Intelligence section. Without observing professional protocol, he opened the door, and marched in. "Doctor Nørgaard."

Within the hour, Nørgaard and Rodriquez were briefing the Secretary of State, Mister Cordell Hull. Though not a scientist, Secretary Hull quickly grasped the scientific and political importance of Rodriquez's analysis of Smith's message, and he understood the compelling need to get an agent into Abyssinia quickly to retrieve samples of this radioactive ore.

Rodriquez stated, "If this ore proves to be as rich in uranium-235 as Fermi reported, it is critical that we keep this mineral away from the fascists and their Nazi allies. We know, from open publications and secret sources, that the Germans are conducting extensive experiments in nuclear fission using uranium-235. Their goal is to design a bomb of tremendous power—a power beyond our comprehension."

Secretary Hull looked purposefully at Rodriquez. "Very well. We'll get an operation underway now. Rodriquez, you are the action officer. I'll need a weekly report; sooner for critical happenings. Nørgaard, make sure that Rodriquez has full support."

"Yes, sir."

"What's the intelligence code word for this operation, Nørgaard?"

"Next on the list is 'Gamma.'"

"Done. Rodriquez, we need to know what Doctor Sofia Russo's intentions are. Is she returning to Abyssinia to continue her explorations? If so, when?"

Nørgaard responded, "We'll draft a cable this afternoon for Smith. He has an excellent network and I suspect we'll have the answers in a few days."

Hull leaned back in his chair and let his mind sort the scope and potential risks of this operation. "I'll check with the research desk to see what the Italians are doing in East Africa and what restrictions they have imposed in that area." As a last thought, he asked, "Can she get a visa to enter Abyssinia and continue her work?"

"Probably not."

Hull stood and said, "I'll arrange a meeting with the President. He'll want to know what we're doing and why. Stand by. You're going with me. I'll let you know the time. In the meantime, develop a preliminary operation plan."

ↄ

The Oval Office, the White House. Late afternoon, 13 August 1937.

President Roosevelt listened with sharp interest as Secretary Hull, Nørgaard, and Rodriquez laid out the importance of Smith's report and the details of the Gamma operational plan. Hull concluded, "What we don't know is how much of this uranium-235 is in the cave and surrounding area."

After a moment of reflection, the president addressed Doctor Max von Bloum, the Science Advisory Board head. "Max, what's your take?"

"Mister President, this intelligence is an amazing revelation, and perhaps a golden opportunity for us to get the type of ore we need and to scoop the Nazis. There are a couple of scientists at the University of Chicago experimenting with the isotope uranium-235 to develop a working atomic pile. We know the theory of nuclear fission, but we're just beginning to understand the complex engineering required. A sustained nuclear reaction could be a source of energy— perhaps a tremendous amount of energy. And, if packaged correctly, could make an atomic bomb that would obliterate an entire city." He paused to regroup his thoughts. "Nonetheless, 235 is the key. We need all we can find and we must keep it away from the dictators."

"Max, how soon will we begin to solve the engineering hurdles?"

"Unknown. Several years at a minimum."

"If there is going to be an atomic bomb, we'll have it first. Let's get involved with those fellows in Chicago. Do what's needed."

President Roosevelt then addressed Harry Hopkins, his close personal advisor. "Well, Harry, looks as if we've got another full-scale, foreign situation on our hands. What kind of political blow back can we expect if this operation goes awry?"

"Mister President, the worst-case scenario is we'll lose our agent. Doctor Russo under torture will tell all and then disappear. And, the Nazis will have the uranium-235 ore. Mussolini will make loud noises of no significance."

President Roosevelt and his close staff understood there was an international political situation simmering under the surface, and that in a few years, a world war would be in the offing.

The president whirled his wheelchair around, gazed at the grounds outside the Oval Office, and drew deeply from the cigarette inserted in his ever-present holder. In a couple of minutes, he asked Secretary Hull, "What are Doctor Russo's politics? Is she returning to Abyssinia to work on her dig? If so, when? Can we count on her to cooperate? Will the Italians give her a visa? If not, do we have any leverage?"

"Mister President, we're working on most of those very questions now. We should have answers in a few days. I'll brief you as soon as we have the complete package." He looked at Rodriquez. "Doctor Rodriquez is our action officer."

"Have we got an agent on station to handle this operation?"

"No, sir. None who are qualified. I suggest that we ask Walter Gregory. Several times over the past few years he's conducted undercover missions for our Bureau of Intelligence and Research; his work is always first-class. For this operation, he has excellent bona fides as a petroleum engineer, amateur archeologist, and photographer of ancient sites, and he currently has an active Secret clearance."

"That's Wallis Gregory's oldest boy—that oil man in West Texas?"

"Exactly."

"Very well. Secretary Hull, draft a letter for my signature: ask Gregory to come to Washington to visit you for a briefing on a special operation. We need him to serve our country one more time."

The president addressed Doctor Rodriquez. "Personally deliver my letter to Walter Gregory. Hint at the importance of the operation, but no details. We'll brief him on Gamma only when he agrees to accept the assignment. Leave tomorrow. I'll have the Army Air Corps take you to Texas in one of their new Boeing YB-17 airplanes. They'll fly up from Langley Field and meet you at Bolling Field over at Anacostia around 1000 hours."

The president said, firmly, "I conditionally approve operation Gamma. I'll reserve final approval pending satisfactory resolution of my questions and Gregory's assignment acceptance. Keep me posted."

જ

Walter's office, Gregory Ranch, near Odessa, Texas. 14 August 1937.

"I've got a business to run." Walter sounded slightly miffed at Doctor Rodriquez. "This isn't the time for me to run all over the world on a lark." Walter stared at Rodriquez. "I've read the president's letter but it's void of import. You've told me nothing of significance except, 'Our country needs you on a matter of national interest.' You've been mimicking the president's entreaties."

Walter turned and looked out his window; he wondered what was going on. He saw the Boeing YB-17 parked next to his Lockheed Electra. *That's impressive. That bomber is the newest the Army has. What are these fellows up to?* His mind raced and he began to see a bigger picture. *I'm being selfish. Obviously this assignment is of great consequence. But they've got other agents. Why me?* The bigger issue for Walter was his brother Mark. Under Elizabeth's care he was improving, but the wounds went deeper than his missing legs. He suffered from phantom leg syndrome. Mark had been as adventurous as his brother and enjoyed hiking and skiing. He had even spent time as a wildcatter on the oil rigs. "How is it even possible for me to be a man without my legs?" he had asked Walter only a few days ago. Walter knew that his brother needed him and might even be resentful of his ability to take off on a globe-trotting adventure—but his country needed him.

The president wants me, and they've sent their latest and finest air-plane to transport his messenger. He owed it to Rodriguez to at least hear him out. He said, "Doctor Rodriquez, you are aware that I have an active Secret clearance. Surely, you can tell me more about this assignment."

Slightly chagrined, Rodriquez responded, "Mister Gregory, you are not yet cleared for this intelligence assignment. If you agree to accept it, you will be sworn into the program in Washington."

Walter realized that he was not going to get any more informa-tion from Rodriquez. Before he could make a commitment, how-ever, he needed to see Mark.

გა

Elizabeth was sitting with Mark when Walter entered the room. He could see that their relationship had grown beyond that of nurse and patient. There was a genuine affection between the two. The possibility of love for his brother made Walter more confident about the conversation he needed to have with Mark.

"I'll leave you two alone to talk," Elizabeth offered.

"No," Mark said. "Anything my brother has to say to me, you should hear as well."

"Yes, dear," Elizabeth demurred.

Walter was impressed. Mark was in charge. Maybe his worries were unfounded. After speaking with both of them, Walter had no doubt as to how he should proceed. Mark shared his patriotic convictions and insisted that Walter take the assignment.

Walter returned to his office. Smiling faintly, he said, "What the hell? Okay. I'm in. What's the deal?"

Doctor Rodriguez met Walter's eyes with intensity. "I must caution you that from this point on, everything we say is classified Top Secret."

"Okay."

Rodriquez, with a faint smile, said, "Telephone the Italian Embassy in D.C. Tell them you want to continue your archeology work from 1933 to search for King Ezana's tomb in Abyssinia, and you want to apply for a visa."

"That's nonsense. No one gets into Abyssinia nowadays. It's under martial law."

"Exactly." He grinned broadly. "We'll take it from there. You'll get the visa." He began to pack his papers in his portfolio. "Be at the State Department in no less than seven days. Ask for me."

A few minutes later, Walter stood in front of his Electra as the Boeing bomber lifted off and went 'wheels up.' The Doppler roar of the four massive engines filled his heart with pride.

chapter six

State Department, Washington, D.C. 16 August 1937.

Cordell Hull invited the Italian ambassador, Carlo Spada, to the State Department for a business lunch. The agenda was to discuss a couple of small items that they needed to resolve. Spada was a longtime career diplomat with an acute sixth sense that ferreted out the underlying truth in diplomatic communications.

Hull spoke in measured phrases during the lunch, a fine Italian wine, green salad, pasta, roast lamb, and spumoni for dessert. Hull focused the conversation on the Italian occupation of Abyssinia. Towards the end of lunch, Hull said in his most friendly voice, "Ambassador Spada, may I ask you for a favor?"

The short, stocky ambassador looked quizzically at Hull. He was perplexed. Throughout the lunch, Hull had been on a sly diplomatic offensive. Spada understood and responded, "Of course, Secretary Hull. We're always eager to enrich the Kingdom of Italy's enduring friendship with the United States. How can I be of service?"

Hull forced a large smile and, without ado, simply responded, "Thanks, Ambassador. The son of a dear friend, Walter Gregory, an amateur archeologist, wants to return to Abyssinia to continue his search for King Ezana's tomb. Will you arrange a visa for him?"

Spada leaned back in his chair and stroked his Van Dyke beard as he evaluated Hull's request. "What you ask is most difficult. All of Italian East Africa, Abyssinia, Eritrea, and Italian Somaliland, are under martial law and only those with important government business are allowed into these areas."

Spada withdrew a silver case from his coat pocket, selected one of the cigarettes, and lit it with his silver lighter. He inhaled deeply, tilted his head back, and slowly exhaled, letting the smoke spiral upward. He sat upright. "Secretary Hull, please understand that Marshal Rodolfo Graziani, the First Viceroy and Governor General of Italian East Africa, must authorize such a visa request. Final approval is the prerogative of our Minister of Foreign Affairs in Rome, Gian Galeazzo Ciano."

Spada leaned closer to Hull and continued, "I'm sure you are aware that Ciano is *Il Duce* Benito Mussolini's son-in-law. Serious questions will be asked. And I'll come under suspicion. You can see why I'm reluctant to honor your request."

"Ambassador Spada, I understand your position. However, my request for this visa has the authorization of President Roosevelt. For many years, Gregory's father has donated large sums to the Democratic Party and, as we say in the West, he is 'calling in his marker.'"

"I see. Unfortunately, your rationale is of no concern to the Italian government. We avoid meddling in our host government's politics." He paused to communicate carefully his next response. His face was contorted into an expression of distrust mixed with curiosity. "I need more details on why your president is anxious for this Gregory fellow to enter our Abyssinia." Spada stubbed out his cigarette in the ashtray, narrowed his eyes, and with a faint, contemptuous smile remarked, "Perhaps there is more to your request than I understand. Is that not so?"

"Ambassador Spada, Carlo, I am shocked that you would suspect my motives. We've been associates for several years and there is sincere trust between us."

"Mister Secretary, I trust you; however, some small indiscretions in the past by your Bureau of Intelligence and Research have caused me some embarrassment with my government." With a rough edge in his voice, he continued, "You recall that incident last year in Eritrea when your agent and that MI6 female were arrested for smuggling guns to the Muslim guerillas. Fortunately, both had diplomatic immunity and we quietly dropped the incident. Then, I recall the contretemps in Tobruk…."

Hull interrupted without an apology. "Here's what I know about Walter Gregory's proposed expedition. In his 1933 search, Gregory found tantalizing clues about the location of King Ezana's tomb a few miles northeast of Axum. His goal in this proposed exploration is to exploit these clues, narrow the search area, and find the tomb."

Spada, with an exaggerated gesture, responded, "A noble goal, I concede. But, I wonder, what's the subtext of this expedition?"

"Ambassador Spada, Gregory does not work for me or for any part of my government. As an archeologist, he is committed to finding this tomb. It's the thrill of the search and the reward for success. That's all there is to my request for his visa."

Spada smiled thinly, "I understand." He knew Hull was lying.

Hull replied, "Consider that the discovery of King Ezana's grave would be a wonderful coup for Italy. This discovery would mean international publicity for Mussolini's government."

"Yes, as you say. " Spada paused for effect, then continued, "It would be an important discovery for the archeological community, but, Secretary Hull, I cannot in good conscience forward your request." He rose and extended his hand. "Thank you for a delightful lunch. Next time it will be pasta in my embassy. Good day."

Hull rose, shook hands with the ambassador, and escorted Spada to the door. "A moment, Ambassador, please."

Spada paused and turned to his host. "Yes, Mister Secretary?"

"May I suggest we step into the garden for a private conversation?"

Realizing that he had successfully finessed Hull into possibly revealing the untold details of Gregory's proposed expedition, Spada replied, "Of course."

The pair strolled quietly in the rose garden for a few minutes. Hull gently touched Spada's arm. "Ambassador Spada, my longtime friend, let us talk off the record."

"Very well," Spada responded.

"We both realize that a world war is looming. The Axis powers will have initial success. However, in the long term, the democracies will prevail and Italy, as a major partner in the Axis, will suffer severely during the war and afterwards, as reprisals begin."

"Mister Secretary, I agree with you; however, I'm helpless."

"My sympathies, Ambassador Spada." Hull paused for several beats. "I'll be frank with you. We know for an absolute certainty that you are opposed to the fascist regime, have made several attempts to contact others of a similar belief, and have tried to form an underground resistance."

Spada stopped cold in his tracks, his face turned pale, and small beads of perspiration formed on his forehead. Trembling, he mumbled, "How?"

"We also have confirmed that the Italian secret police have opened a dossier on you. On your return to Italy, the OVRA will arrest you and your family."

Spada collapsed onto a steel lawn chair and buried his face in his hands.

Hull sat down next to him. A few minutes later, as Spada composed himself, Hull continued," I have an offer for you, my friend."

"What offer? What are you saying?"

"Here is what I propose: Get this visa for Gregory and we will offer you and your family sanctuary. We'll put you into a witness protection program and deposit two hundred thousand dollars for you in a secret bank account."

"You are serious? This is true?"

"You have my word."

Ambassador Spada did not speak. He fumbled for a cigarette. Hull said, "Permit me."

"Thank you, Mister Secretary." Spada began to leave.

"By the by, Ambassador Spada, there is another matter of minor import that we would ask you to consider."

Resigned and slightly irritated, Spada in a too-harsh voice said, "You will send me to an OVRA prison with your minor matters." He drew deeply on his cigarette, and the exhaled smoke drifted lazily about the still garden. He threw up his hands in resignation. "With your permission, Ambassador Hull, I sit."

Hull sat beside the Italian ambassador, and in his matter-of-fact voice commented, "We understand that *Il Duce's* son-in-law, *Conte Gain Galeazzo Ciano*, the Italian Minister of Foreign Affairs, is a *sub rosa* associate of yours."

Spada gasped in awe. He sputtered hurriedly, "Respectfully, Ambassador, you are a blackguard." He paused to recoup. "I admire your intelligence organization. *Mannaggia dial!*"

Hull ignored the mild invective. "We are led to believe that your distinguished citizen Doctor Sofia Savoy Russo, the second cousin of King Victor Emmanuel Savoy, shortly may apply for a visa to enter Abyssinia to continue her archeology work near Axum. We would be most pleased, and financially grateful, if she were granted the visa without ado."

Understanding fully his untenable position, Spada asked, "How grateful? "

"One hundred thousand dollars grateful."

"For me to paper my OVRA cell, no doubt."

"Discretion, Ambassador Spada. Leave no fingerprints."

‿

State Department, Washington D.C. 21 August 1937.

Walter stood at attention; his left hand was on a King James Bible, and his right hand was upright, the arm bent at the elbow. He said, "I agree." He signed the document that acknowledged he had received the briefing and that he understood the legal requirements and penalties associated with this code-word Gamma intelligence program.

Secretary Hull shook Walter's hand and welcomed him to the Gamma program. Rodriquez said to Walter, "Come with me. We're going to a secure room. I'm going to brief you on the details of your assignment and outline the essential elements of information on this mission."

Two hours later, Rodriquez handed Gregory his passport with an Italian visa for Abyssinia, valid for ninety days; twenty-one, used gold certificates in one-thousand-dollar denominations, thirty-one, one hundred dollar bills, a raft of Italian Lira and Egyptian pounds, and a calf skin money belt; and an airline ticket on a Pan American Clipper to Lisbon. Rodriquez shook Gregory's hand and quipped, "Good luck."

ော

That night in the Willard Hotel, Walter reviewed the key points of his assignment. He thought back to Rodriquez's briefing: "Your cover is that you are an amateur archeologist whose goal is to find and photograph the tombs of ancient Abyssinian kings—continuing your work started in 1933. Once there, you are to meet Doctor Sofia Russo at the Goha Hotel in Axum, befriend her, and suggest that the two of you share clues and resources to find King Ezana's burial place. After gaining her confidence and trust, you are to entice her to reveal the location of the cave on the pretext that you have a serious interest in the parchments she found. Get samples of the radioactive ore from inside the cave and from several locations nearby, and then smuggle them out of the Italian-controlled areas."

Walter reviewed the name of his local contact and the locations of the dead drops in Axum for sending messages to Rodriquez. With a *National Geographic®* map of East Africa spread on his bed, he reviewed the various escape routes Rodriquez had suggested. He memorized the British and American resources that were tasked with helping him, and how to communicate with them. Lastly, he cut all notes relating to his assignment into small strips and flushed them down the toilet.

❦

A few days later, at Floyd Bennett Field, Walter boarded a Pan American World Airways Transatlantic Flying Boat for a flight to Lisbon, via Bermuda and the Azores. En route, he read the Pocketbook edition of Lost Horizon. After an overnight stay in the Santa Maria Hotel, he boarded an Imperial Airways' Short Empire Flying Boat for a two-day flight to Alexandria, via Marseille, Naples, Brindisi, and Athens. On arrival, he checked into the Montazah Hotel. Exhausted, he skipped dinner, tossed down a double whiskey, and collapsed on the feather-soft bed.

Early the next morning, Walter boarded a first-class compartment on Egypt National Railways for the six-hour trip to Cairo. On arrival, Walter checked into the Shepheard Hotel, told the bell desk to take his luggage to his suite, strolled into the bar, and ordered a double bourbon. Too tired for small talk, he ignored the other guests, and tossed down his drink. At the other end of the bar, a handsome *une femme d'un certain âge* smiled coyly at him. Tempted to engage her, he spotted a large diamond ring on her left hand. His better judgment prevailed. On this mission, the last thing he needed was to deal with an irate husband. He signed his bill, entered the restaurant, and ordered a large steak dinner with all the trimmings.

❦

The following afternoon, Walter visited the Cairo Museum. He strode into the African section and introduced himself to Doctor Samira el Aslam.

"Thank you for visiting me, Mister Gregory. How may I be of service?"

"I am an amateur archeologist and have been on several digs in East Africa searching for King Ezana's tomb." With a straight face and intense eyes, Walter began to fabricate his story. "In my 1933 expedition, I found several enticing clues about its location— somewhere northwest of Axum. I've read some of your papers and articles on the ancient burial rites in this area and respect your expertise. In the next day or so, I'm going to Abyssinia to continue my search. Perhaps you could help by offering current information and some advice."

Samira looked at Walter with incredulity. "Mister Gregory, no one gets into Abyssinia. The Italians have a tight clamp on all of their East African possessions …." He leaned forward on his desk and in a hard, straightforward voice, said, "My advice is, stay away. No good can come of such a visit. Their secret police are ruthless and have *carte blanche* to keep order." He relaxed and asked in a softer voice, "You have a visa?"

"Yes, sir. Good for ninety days."

"Pray tell, how did you persuade the Italians to issue you a visa?"

"Officials in our State Department arranged it. My father donates large funds to President Roosevelt's Democratic Party—very large sums. My dad asked the President to intercede and help me get the visa." He continued, "I don't know what strings the President pulled, but within a couple of weeks the Italian Embassy stamped my passport."

Samira was no fool and knew that Gregory's story was chicanery. He wondered what the Americans were doing in Abyssinia— something to do with the forthcoming war, perhaps. He had no sympathy for the fascists and decided that he'd accept Gregory's tale and help him. "That's an amazing story. Congratulations."

"Thank you, Doctor. But I can't accept your advice not to enter Abyssinia. I'm committed to this dig."

"Actually, your visit is quite a coincidence. Last May, a dear friend of mine, Doctor Sofia Savoy Russo, returned from a dig near Axum. She was also searching for King Ezana's tomb. She stopped in Cairo for a few days and we had a pleasant visit. You've heard of her?"

"Unfortunately, no," he lied. "I'd like to meet her and exchange information and ideas. How may I contact her?"

"She is a professor of archeology at the University of Rome. In her latest correspondence, she said she is trying to get a visa to continue her work in Abyssinia. Perhaps you'll see her in Axum."

"That's a grand idea," Walter said too eagerly. "I'm looking forward to meeting her."

"By chance, Doctor Russo made an amazing discovery. Let me show you." He withdrew one of the shards and a sample of the parchment fragments from his desk drawer. "Doctor Russo found some very old amphorae in a hidden cave. Many were broken and their parchment contents scattered."

He scanned the shards with the Geiger counter. "See how this instrument detects the relatively high radioactivity from the dust on the shard?" Samira watched intently for Walter's reaction. Soon Samira had confirmed his suspicions about this American fellow.

෴

On the way to his hotel, Walter, knowing that the OVRA was listening to all telephone calls into and out of the American Embassy, reviewed the stratagem for communicating with his State Department contact. He stopped at a cafe and called Adam Smith.

Smith answered on the fourth ring, *"Pronto."*

Gregory paused two beats, covered the receiver with his handkerchief, and said in a squeaky, affected English voice, "It is I."

"I understand, Sir."

"All's well."

"Ciao."

❧

The next morning, Walter boarded a Imperial Airways Handley Page H.P. 45, four-engine biplane for the one-thousand mile, fourteen–hour trip to Khartoum. At each of the three stops in between, Walter deplaned and walked for several minutes to ease the stiffness invading his body.

That evening in Khartoum, Walter checked into the Acropole Hotel. After several days of intense travel, he was exhausted. He collapsed on the sumptuous bed in his suite for a deep and refreshing sleep. He planned to stay in Khartoum for several days to recoup.

Late the next afternoon, the scorching desert sun and the intense humidity from the White and Nile Rivers made the day almost intolerable. Walter, with his linen suit coat draped over his arm, walked into the Italian Legation office to arrange air transportation to Addis Ababa.

chapter seven

University of Rome. 22 July 1937.

It was quiet on the University campus and Sofia was in her office plotting a strategy to renew her visa for Abyssinia. She was driven to return and complete a thorough investigation and inventory of the amphorae and parchments in the cave, and to resume her search for the tomb of King Ezana.

Her most perplexing problem was to devise a strategy to remove these artifacts safely and responsibly without alerting the OVRA. She considered storing them secretly in Axum, but she soon rejected this option because she knew that OVRA agents would be tracking her constantly. She was at a loss because no matter what she devised, she realized she could not keep her activities confidential. Sofia realized that her only reasonable option was to leave the artifacts in the cave, which she was loath to do.

Sofia realized there was no point in applying for a visa to Abyssinia via the routine channels. The bureaucrats would stall and eventually reject her application. Her only option was to appeal to her cousin, King Victor Emmanuel III, from the House of Savoy, and to General Rodolfo Graziani, who was a close family friend and comrade-in-arms of her deceased husband.

Sofia wrote a short letter to the King's personal secretary asking for a meeting with her cousin. Within a few days, she received a tele-phone call from the appointment secretary telling her that she could meet with the King for twenty minutes that same afternoon. "Please be here at 1600 hours."

She was pleased that her request had been honored so quickly. As soon as she hung up the telephone, she dashed to her dressing room to decide what to wear to the meeting. Widowhood had diminished her social life, so her choices were limited. But her eyes fell on an elegant afternoon gown in a rich, blue silk crepe, which had a matching coat with a plush, white, fox collar. She had worn it to a reception at the palace a couple of years earlier, but she doubted that Victor Emmanuel would recall or had even noticed it. It had a matching hat, a frivolous confection from a famous Parisian milliner which had been the height of fashion when she bought it, but by now was no doubt hopelessly *passé*. Sofia reminded herself that her cousin had never been interested in fashion and the opinions of his chamberlains were of no importance to her or her mission. She would wear the outfit with the long strand of South Sea pearls that had been a wedding gift from her father-in-law. She was confident this would be suitable for her meeting with the King. Since there wasn't enough time for her to visit a hairdresser, she decided to pull her hair back into a chignon. Although it was a rather severe style for the chosen gown, Sofia knew that the hairdo would accentuate the fine bones of her face, which her family had always insisted resembled those of several of Europe's most distinguished noble families.

By the time she stepped into the taxi, Sofia presented the mien of an aristocratic lady of fashion. Sofia returned the taxi driver's attention to her dress with a cool nod, all the while realizing that inside her long, white, kid gloves her hands were trembling. Normally, she was completely calm around the King. She had, after all, moved in his social circle her entire life, and usually she found her diminutive, fussy cousin, at worst, a tolerable bore. She knew her future as an archeologist, in the current political climate, depended on today's meeting with him. Old family ties were irrelevant, only politics were important.

She had arranged to arrive at the palace a few minutes early for their scheduled meeting. Protocol demanded that one never make royalty wait, not even second cousins. Upon arrival, she was escorted into a large salon to wait until the King was ready to receive her. She took deep breaths to calm herself, and looked idly around the room, taking in the quartet of Roman marble busts that stood between the high French windows and the portraits of royal ancestors (some of them also Sofia's ancestors) that covered the walls. A superb Madonna and Child, which was obviously one of da Vinci's masterworks, sat on its own gilded easel next to the inside wall of the room. Most of the furniture came from the eighteenth century and was covered with silk damask in the sweet pastels of the era. She was examining an elaborate Baroque ceiling fresco by Giovanni Lanfranco when the chamberlain interrupted her thoughts.

"His Majesty will see you now, *Signora.*"

Sofia rose and followed him through a door at the end of the room and through another equally elegant salon. A footman stood before a door at the far end of the room and knocked lightly as Sofia and the chamberlain approached. Just as they came to the door, he opened it silently. The chamberlain stepped through the door and to the side. Bowing deeply, he faced the King and announced, "*Signora* Sofia Savoy Russo.*"

They were in the King's personal sitting room. It was a smaller compartment at the corner of the palace, with vast windows along two walls. It held a number of impressive art treasures, but the furniture was covered with slightly faded chintz and the air was redolent of the cigarettes to which the King was addicted, and of the citrus and bergamot-scented eau de Cologne that Sofia had always associated with him.

As the King rose from his desk, Sofia fell into a deep curtsy.

"My dear cousin!" Victor Emmanuel cried as he walked toward her and took her hand. "What a delightful interruption to a dreary day." He pulled her up from her curtsy and reached up to kiss her cheeks. "What a pleasure to see you, my dear." He led her to a settee and waved the chamberlain away with the instruction, "Bring us tea," as the man backed out the door. "Please be seated, Sofia."

Today the sixty-eight-year-old, five-foot-tall King was dressed in a lightweight, blue suit with a red and green striped tie. His shrewd eyes were a dull brown. His face was fine-drawn, taut, and sporting a well-groomed chevron mustache, and his affect was that of an un-happy man nearly overcome with worry and discontent. "Now, my dear, tell me what brings you to brighten an old man's tedium."

Sofia, ensconced in a sumptuous, leather settee, commented, "It has been far too long since we met, Your Grace. As I recall, we talked briefly at the reception for the new German ambassador—a few months after my husband's funeral."

The King's right eye cocked into a quizzical look. "You are cor-rect. It has been far too long."

The chamberlain returned with a silver tea service. He poured the steaming lapsang souchong into delicate porcelain cups deco-rated with the House of Savoy emblem.

The King continued, "I've been remiss in not having you for dinner to discuss our family and how we are faring under *Il Duce* Mussolini's fascist regime." He raised both eyes with a mock salute. "I'll make a note and we'll meet again shortly."

Sofia smiled politely. "I'll be honored, and look forward to your invitation." She sipped her tea, and with a hint of embarrassment in her voice said, "Your Grace, I am here to ask a favor—a very large and difficult favor."

The King, obviously curious, nodded for her to continue.

Quickly, Sofia outlined her dilemma. For all his flaws, Victor Emmanuel had a strong respect for history and archeology, and Sofia knew she could trust his discretion in the matter of the cave and its precious contents. She concluded with a request that he assist her in acquiring the necessary visa to return to Abyssinia.

The King sipped the tea, and then carefully placed his cup and saucer on the tea table in front of him. "My dear Sofia, *Il Duce* and his fascists don't pay much attention to me these days, and I have virtually no authority. I'm but a useful icon for him and his Black Shirt associates. However, I will ask our Minister of Foreign Affairs, Count Gian Galeazzo Ciano, to consider issuing your visa. But frankly, Sofia, I don't have much confidence in success."

The King sighed deeply and took a cigarette from a gilded box on the side table. He lit it and inhaled deeply. "And, even if Ciano approves the visa, there is another major checkpoint: General Rodolfo Graziani, Marshal of Italian East Africa, will have to approve."

"Marshal Graziani approved my earlier visa. I'll write him a personal letter revealing that I uncovered credible and convincing clues about King Ezana's tomb on my last dig. I'll tell him that I have reasonable confidence that I'll find the tomb, if only he will approve my visa so that I can return to Abyssinia and continue my work."

❧

Several weeks later, Sofia was polishing the final draft of a paper about her dig earlier in the year. The jangling telephone interrupted her intense concentration. Annoyed by the disruption, she grabbed the receiver and said a little too harshly, "*Pronto*. Doctor Sofia Russo speaking."

"*Buon giorno*, Doctor Russo. This is Tazio Di Pasqua, King Emmanuel's personal secretary. I would suggest that you report to the office of the Foreign Minister tomorrow morning to get your passport with a ninety-day visa for Abyssinia."

Surprised and childishly happy, Sofia responded, "*Si. Si.* I'll be there. *Grazie molto, Signore* Di Pasqua. *Grazie tanto! Addio.*" She made the sign of the Cross and sent a silent prayer of thanks to her patron saint, Sophia, the martyr of ancient Rome.

❦

Sofia, en route to Abyssinia. 20 August 1937.

A week later, Sofia boarded a Greek tramp steamer out of Anzio, bound for Tobruk in Cyrenaica. She was the only passenger aboard for the five-day voyage. She had a small but comfortable stateroom in the officers' quarters. The crew, a mix of nationalities, treated her with courtesy, and the captain ensured that the steward catered promptly to her requests. Aiming to please the beautiful female passenger, the Armenian cook prepared meals to her taste. During the voyage, she worked on and reworked a plan to evacuate the artifacts, but none seemed satisfactory. There were just too many unknowns.

At the dock in Tobruk, a junior air corps officer in his crisp summer uniform took off his pith helmet, saluted, and asked Sofia as she stepped off the gangplank, "You are *Signora* Sofia Savoy Russo?"

"*Si, Signore.*" Sofia's heart raced and fear appeared in her eyes. *Am I being arrested already? What have I done?*

"*Buon giorno, Signora* Russo. I am *Tenente* Fione Lazzari." The twenty-three-year-old officer explained that he would escort her to *Regia Aeronautica* airfield, about ten miles south.

His bright green eyes scanned the beautiful and poised woman standing before him. With a racing pulse and a slight choke in his voice, he continued, "My driver will handle your luggage and equipment." He took Sofia by the arm and led her to a military sedan. "Please sit in the back, *Signora.*" Lazzari checked to see that her gear was stored correctly in the trunk, entered the front passenger seat, and told the driver, "To the airfield." The automobile moved at a fast pace, and *Tenente* Lazzari offered no explanation and remained stealthily quiet.

Sofia's mind raced with possibilities as the automobile sped southward. Although she wore light summer clothing, the oppressive desert heat made her slightly light headed, which compounded her distress. Eventually, she roused her courage and demanded, "*Tenente* Lazzari, what is happening? Why have you arrested me?"

Tenente Lazzari turned to face Sofia. "*Mi scuso, Signora.* You are not under arrest. I've been ordered to escort you to the officers' quarters at our air base. We should arrive in a few minutes."

With increasing anxiety she snapped, "Who ordered you? And to what purpose?"

"My squadron leader, *Signora*. He was responding to a Priority message from Marshal General Rudolfo Graziani. The Marshal has ordered us to look after you until the airplane arrives."

Now more confused and afraid than ever, Sofia was near tears. "I don't understand. What airplane?"

Trying to alleviate her obvious distress, *Tenente* Lazzari responded in a soft, empathetic voice, A CANT Z Tri-Motor Bomber modified to transport passengers will arrive in a few days from Addis Ababa. You have a reserved seat on the return flight."

Somewhat mollified, yet still troubled, Sofia stated, "*Grazie.* But I still don't understand. How did Marshal General Graziani know my schedule?"

With deep concern in his eyes, *Tenente* Lazzari responded, "*Signora*, may I speak frankly? You speak English?"

Sofia leaned forward and forced the issue. "Of course, I speak English and I encourage you to be totally honest with me."

Lazzari spoke in English, "My driver knows only Italian." He turned to see if the driver responded. Satisfied that he had not, he continued in a whisper. "I'm not exactly sure what is happening." He paused to recoup his thoughts. "I know the OVRA drafted the message for the General's signature. The message was on the OVRA's exclusive red paper and was sent via our top secret 'back channel,' which is used only for critical intelligence matters."

Stunned, Sofia fell back into the seat and sighed deeply as the automobile rushed deeper into the desert. She could not understand the OVRA's uproar over her return to Axum. Now a spasm of fear gripped her. Though she was not under arrest, she was certainly in OVRA custody. She began to sob silently as she realized that all her plans for the dig and cave exploration probably were for naught. *Was asking King Emanuel for help the error that had alerted the OVRA to the archeology project? Why are they interested? What is happening?*

They approached the main gate to the airfield and the military police waved them through without question. Again, she was puzzled. It was most unusual for anyone to pass unchallenged into a critical military facility in this wartime environment. "*Signora.*" *Tenente* Lazzari spoke in English. "Please excuse me. Even though I am an aviator, my assignment is to be your escort while at this base. You are to remain in your quarters. I will bring your meals and anything else you require."

Resigned, Sofia commented, "I understand." As she calmed herself she asked, "Tell me *Tenente* Lazzari, why is the OVRA so interested in me? I have no foreign connections. My father, husband, and son died for Italy. Surely I am no security risk."

Uncomfortable at the scene and his onerous task, Lazzari said softly, "Frankly, I don't know. I suspect that the OVRA has something to hide."

The roar of several multi-engine aircraft taking off effectively cut off all conversation.

A few minutes later Sofia heard, "*Signora*, we are here. Your quarters are that number-one bungalow." He looked away uncomfortably and said, "I will be in number two. When I may be of service, just call me on the intercommunication system—the box is on the desk. I urge you not to wander outside without me as your escort."

Mentally and physically exhausted, Sofia murmured, "*Capisco, Tenente* Lazzari." At the door, she took his hand and said, "*Grazie* for your courtesy and integrity."

Except for the daunting heat, the next few days were pleasant enough for Sofia. Occasionally during the night, she heard muffled explosions in the distance. With Lazzari at her side, she had free access to most of the airfield. Early evening walks around the housing and public areas revived her spirits. Lazzari always had a ready smile and was attentive, polite, and catered quickly to her requests. At dinnertime, he would bring a bottle of wine with the food and eat with her in her quarters. They chatted amicably on a host of topics. Lazzari was a graduate of the University of Pisa and had majored in contemporary literature. F. Scott Fitzgerald was his favorite author and *The Beautiful and the Damned* was his favorite novel.

Four days later, during their evening walk, Lazzari said, "Good news, *Signora* Russo. The CANT Z will arrive later this evening. Tomorrow morning, you'll be on your way to Abyssinia."

Sofia grabbed his arm, "Is this true?"

"*Si.* The CANT will be serviced tonight and be ready to whisk you away," he said with a touch of sadness. "Be ready at 0600 hours. I'll drive you to the terminal."

"*Fione*, you've been a dear and I shall remember you." She put her arms around him and kissed him on both cheeks.

He backed away slightly, and she saw a few tears on his cheeks. She was embarrassed to realize that Lazzari had fallen in love with her. "We won't say *arrivederci*. We'll meet again under more agreeable circumstances one day soon."

❧

Goha Hotel, Axum, Abyssinia. 1 September 1937.

Sofia walked into the lobby of the Goha Hotel in Axum. She was exhausted and slightly disheveled from her long, cramped, and noisy twenty-hour flight with stops in Cairo, Aswan, Khartoum, and finally Addis Ababa. A hired coach drove her to Axum, and in a few hours she was greeted with an enthusiastic, "Welcome, *Signora* Doctor Russo," from the desk clerk, Joseph Kabede. "We've been expecting you. Your suite is ready, and the bellman will handle your luggage and equipment."

Sofia greeted Kabede warmly and said, "Thank you, Joseph. I'm glad to be back. You've been well, I hope?"

"Yes, thank you. I have your crew standing by and the Auto Union Explorer is fully serviced and ready for you. Here are the keys."

Sofia thanked him and whispered, "I've been followed on my entire journey."

Joseph gave a slight nod towards a fellow who was sitting in a wicker chair at the far end of the lobby. "Your plump OVRA *paisano* is waiting for you. He's been here two days—stinking up the lobby with his presence." He whispered with faux apology and a forced smile, "I am being rude. *Mi scusi, Signora.*"

"He's no friend of mine," she said. "Frankly, I was hoping a crocodile had gotten him."

Ugo Segreti approached the desk and greeted Sofia with a curt, "Come with me, Doctor Russo. You have an appointment with *Colonnello* Jacopo Visco." He grabbed her arm to lead her to his car.

Her face flushed scarlet red, her anger flared, and with an automatic reflex she slapped his hand away from her arm. "If you ever touch me again, I'll kill you."

Undaunted, Segreti flicked open his coat to show his Beretta 38. "You are welcome to try, Doctor Sofia Savoy Russo."

☙

Three hours later, Sofia took a deep drink of Campari, kicked off her shoes, and dropped on her bed fully clothed. She reflected on her meeting with the OVRA supervisor, *Colonnello* Visco. There was to be no change from her last visit. Ugo Segreti would continue to be her "bodyguard," and she would be severely restricted in her movements. Finally, sleep came quickly and deeply.

chapter eight

Goha Hotel, Axum, Abyssinia. 2 September 1937.

When Sofia finally arose, after much-needed sleep, she exercised, bathed, washed and brushed her hair, and unpacked her clothes and equipment. She popped open her survey case, looked under the transit's platform, and saw that her Beretta 32 was still hidden in the cotton cushioning. She withdrew the weapon, and dropped the detachable magazine, which contained seven rounds. Then she snapped the magazine back into the pistol, pulled back the receiver, checked the empty breach, and released the receiver. As it snapped home, it picked up one round from the magazine and chambered it into the barrel. She gently released the cocked hammer to its safe position. She balanced the Beretta in her hand for a few seconds and found the heft of the weapon was reassuring. She wondered if the round in the breach was destined for Segreti.

Around dinnertime, she was almost back to her regular self. She dressed for dinner in a bright-red dress with long sleeves, cinched at the waist, and cut on the bias at her bosom. Around her neck was a thin, white, silk scarf.

She entered the lobby and nodded to the ever-present Joseph Kabede behind the desk. As she strolled into the combined bar/restaurant, she noticed several beautiful, young, Abyssinian women sitting with Italian officers. *That's unusual,* she thought. *I've never seen Abyssinian guests before. I thought they were banned from this Italian-controlled hotel.* Puzzled, she retreated to the desk and quizzed Joseph.

With the faintest contemptuous smile, he leaned toward her and commented in a soft voice, "*Signora*, the management is eager to accommodate our very important Italian guests. We cater to their every whim, at a price, of course."

Sofia smiled at the irony that she, a proper lady of Italian patricians, was staying in a bordello. Her smile was shy and fleeting. However, she was worldly enough to accept the *fait accompli* with good favor.

She entered the dining room and a tall, handsome waiter, impeccably groomed in faux black-and-white dinner dress, addressed her in near-perfect Italian, "Good evening, Doctor *Signora* Russo, welcome to our dining room."

"Good evening to you. A table by the window, please."

He guided Sofia to a small table by a large window that overlooked a lovely garden with peacocks strutting about. She ordered a bottle of spumante.

Segreti followed Sofia, sat at the bar, and ordered a draft beer. He took several swallows, then began to stare at Sofia. She tried to ignore the uncultured clod, but his stare was becoming intensely disturbing to her and those in the room. To ease the embarrassing standoff, she gave a slight nod of her head in acknowledgement. He cracked a twisted smile and returned to his beer.

Almost on cue, the waiter brought a bottle of Piemonte Brachetto, placed it in an ice bucket beside the table, and twirled it back and forth several times. Sofia looked at him quizzically, as this was one of the most sought after, and inordinately expensive, sparkling wines. She wondered if she ought to indulge in this luxury. He expertly popped the cork, poured the bubbling wine into a tall flute, and said, "Joseph sends his compliments, *Signora* Russo."

Somewhat flustered, she responded, "I'm delightfully surprised. How kind. Please give my thanks to Joseph." She took the first sip and the wine sent a shiver of pleasure down her throat. A slow smile invaded her face and she took a deeper drink. A feeling of calm and contentment suffused through her being. The peacock moved to the window and flared his tail as if he were flirting with her.

As Walter Gregory entered the lobby, his rattlesnake-skin boots made a pleasant "twang" on the ceramic floor with each step. He looked about at the guests, who were mostly high-ranking Italian officers, chatting, having their afternoon cocktails, and trying to impress the just-conquered, local women. A few looked up at the Texan. They wondered what the fellow, almost an intruder, was doing in this bucolic setting. Then, just as quickly, they paid no further notice, assuming that the OVRA had cleared him.

Walter ambled to the desk.

Joseph whispered, "*Signora* Russo is in the bar, Mister Gregory."

"Thanks."

Walter walked straight to Sofia's table. "Good afternoon, Doctor *Signora* Russo."

She looked up with dubious eyes at the tall Texan dressed in a tan, short-sleeve, aviator shirt, and neatly pressed khaki trousers. He wore the expensive clothes expertly. In that instant, she liked what she saw.

He held his Stetson in his right hand and continued, "I'm Walter Gregory from Odessa, Texas." Not waiting for her response, he rushed on. "Doctor Samira el Aslam at the Cairo Museum told me about you and your search for King Ezana's tomb and said that you might be in Abyssinia sometime in July." He pulled out a chair from her table and sat down. "May I join you to talk over our mutual interest?" he said with a sly smile.

Sofia was somewhat befuddled by this fellow's intrusive approach, yet she was attracted by his wholesome charm. She managed a stumbling, "Please do."

"Thanks, ma'am." He signaled the waiter and ordered a double bourbon. He looked at her intently and saw that she wore no makeup to decorate her strong, radiant face. He too liked what he saw. He cracked a big smile for Sofia and said, "My, you do look lovely this evening."

Sofia's face flushed at the compliment. It had been several years since a handsome man had flirted with her. "Thank you, Mister Gregory." She smiled, revealing a row of sparkling white teeth. "Please share my wine as you tell me just what our 'mutual interest' might be."

"Thanks for your kind offer, but I can't drink that bubbly stuff. It tickles my nose and I get a sneezing spasm. It must be an allergy or something. I'll stick with bourbon or rye whiskey, with your permission."

Sofia was delighted by this Texan and his frank, yet polite, manner. "Mister Gregory, please drink whatever beverage pleases you."

Walter Gregory presented himself as an amateur, but experienced, archeologist with a long-standing interest in finding King Ezana's tomb. He relayed to her the history of his past archeological expedition seeking out this particular site. To back up his credentials, he told Sofia about his work in Ziviyeh in Persia and Kufa in Mesopotamia.

Sofia now recalled the name Walter Gregory; he was the author of some important papers published in the *Cambridge Archaeological Journal*. He had an excellent reputation as a man of integrity who would never claim discovery of other people's work to burnish his own reputation. Nor would he loot tombs to increase his wealth.

Sofia finished her second flute of wine and felt a sense of well-being. The attentive waiter poured another glass.

"Thank you," she whispered hoarsely.

Unexpectedly, Ugo Segreti approached her table with a glass of beer in his hand. "*Signora* Russo, I see you have a new friend. Introduce me."

With faux courage bolstered by the wine, she rose and stabbed her right index finger toward Segreti's face. "Get away from me, Segreti.

I have no business with you this evening." She grabbed the flute and took a deep drink. "I am in my controlled area and there are no O—V—R—A requirements forcing me to socialize with you. Get out!"

Walter wondered what this argument was about. Instinctively, he supported the indignant Sofia and took an immediate, deep-seated dislike to the boorish fellow. He rose and stood next to Sofia.

Segreti took on an air of righteousness. His tone was authoritative and loud, ensuring everyone in the bar heard him. "Russo, you're in my charge and you don't order me about." With a rush of anger, he cried, *"Comprendere?"*

Walter had heard enough. "Mister Segreti, I reckon Doctor Russo has made her point explicitly clear. It would be prudent for you to leave and tend to your business elsewhere."

Segreti studied Walter with cautious, appraising eyes. He had overplayed his hand and knew that he'd best tread lightly. His face contorted in defeat, and without comment, he turned and went to the bar. He pouted over his beer, promising himself that eventually he would make sure this pair had a serious comeuppance.

Sofia and Walter sat down; each let out a deep sigh, and they gulped down the remainder of their beverages.

The waiter promptly refilled Walter's glass.

Sofia trembled as her adrenalin subsided. "Thanks, Mister Gregory, for standing with me." She took a deep drink of the sparkling wine. "That slob of a man has become the blight of my existence." She forced a tired smile and sipped again. "I'm confident that one day he and I will resolve our adverse issues with violence, and I don't intend to be the vanquished. I suspect that he underestimates my resolve and capability."

"Doctor Russo," Walter addressed her in a calm, empathetic voice. "I'm confused. Who was that fellow, and what charge has he over you?"

A dark frown crept over Sofia's face, and she burst out, "That Segreti, the oaf, is my shadow—my turnkey—a dark shadow from the Italian secret police. He follows me wherever I go—ensuring that I stay within the OVRA's assigned area around my dig. They seem to be concerned that I might find some grim secret."

Walter mulled over her comment, and realized that he needed to play a safe hand with this secret agent, Segreti, lest he compromise his mission. Nonetheless, his curiosity was piqued. *What secrets are the Italians trying to keep hidden in the Axum environs?*

She smiled broadly at her new protector. "Looks as if we've formed a team by default. We'll pool our resources and find King Ezana's tomb—forthwith." Now slightly tipsy, she said, "Call me 'Sofia,' and you'll be 'Walter.'"

"As you say, madam. That's the way a close-knit team works, and we'll have a greater chance of success."

"That's right, Texan," she replied.

Walter gave a slight move of his head toward Segreti.

Sofia was close to slurring her words as she continued her screed on Segreti. "He is obnoxious, a pervert, and a lecherous lout." She sipped her wine. "He makes lewd remarks and thinks he is amusing." Her eyes narrowed. "A few months ago, I caught him staring at me while I was bathing in a stream near my dig. I hit him and threatened to kill him. I loathe him with all my being. He is subhuman." She drained her flute and looked at Walter through watery eyes.

Resigned to the certitude that Segreti would retaliate, she continued, "Walter, I am afraid that this evening you have made a pernicious and powerful enemy. Be careful."

She looks at Walter with roguish eyes and cautions, "As they say in your cowboy moving-pictures, 'Don't draw aces and eights,' and 'Watch your back.'"

"Oh, you like our Westerns," Walter replied with a smile. He was enchanted with this precocious woman, but was not about to show his hand as an American agent or reveal that hidden in his custom-designed, cowhide suitcase was a Colt 38 Special six-shooter and thirty-six bullets.

"Sofia, let's eat. Looks as if the fun is over for this evening. It's long past our dinner time."

Clearly in her cups, she said, "Very well, lead the way, cowboy from Texas, U S of A."

Walter helped Sofia up from the table, took her arm, and guided her to the dining room. A waiter showed them to a table covered with a starched, white cloth, and set for a simple meal.

Walter pulled out a chair for Sofia and sat across from her. She asked for a glass of amaretto and Walter requested plain soda water. He ordered a green salad with olive oil and vinegar on the side, and a basic pasta dish for them both.

Sofia was feeling free and protected for the first time in many years. She stared at Walter with intense eyes, and instead of sipping the sweet liqueur, tossed it down like a shot. *Damn, I like this Texas man*, she thought. *He's good for me.* The alcohol had given her a gentle intoxication. *And I for him.*

Throughout dinner, their conversation was limited to banal small talk. Afterwards, Walter escorted the wobbly Sofia to her suite. At the door she whispered, "Kiss me good night brave knight."

Walter pecked her cheek and said, "Good night, Sofia. Tomorrow we'll plan our dig."

More emphatically, she demanded, "That's no kiss, knight Walter. Try again. This time with some passion."

Walter saw that Sofia was wobbling and about to fall. He grabbed her, carried her into her suite, laid her on the bed, pulled off her shoes, pulled a light blanket over her, turned off the lights, and left.

chapter nine

Goha Hotel, Axum, Abyssinia. 3 September 1937.

The morning alarm that roused Sofia sounded like a cannonade of twelve pounders next to her. She slowly sat upright and took inventory of her aching, post-bubbly body. Her head felt as large as the Graf Zeppelin and the jackhammer pounding in her brain was tortuous. Her mouth was as dry as the Cyrenaica desert.

She focused past the pain, eased out of bed, stripped off her rumpled red dress and accessories, and shuffled slowly to the water closet. She swallowed four aspirins, and swigged a bottle of water in just a few gulps. The shower's hot water seemed to wash away most of her pain, and she wondered what sort of fool she had been last evening. Faint recollections eased into her troubled brain. She remembered her confrontation with Ugo Segreti, and her blatant flirting with that handsome Texan. Her heart skipped a beat and her cheeks reddened.

Later, flushed with embarrassment, Sofia sat across the breakfast table from Walter. She was dressed in her field jacket, tan shirt, khaki trousers, a white neck scarf, and polished high boots. She looked at Walter, and in a soft tone said, "I must apologize for my unbecoming behavior last evening."

Walter was outfitted in his field garb, and had exchanged his cowboy boots for practical, lace-up, calf-length field boots. He looked at the charming lady across from him with understanding eyes. "Not to worry, Sofia. I can't cast a stone. I've made an ass of myself by over-indulging in fermented rye far too many times."

Somewhat mollified, Sofia said, "Thanks for your kind understanding."

"What the heck, next time I'll join you."

Sofia wasn't sure of his meaning, but in any case she liked it.

Walter continued, "My concern, however, is what effect our confrontation with Ugo Segreti will have on our work. Clearly, we've upped the stakes with that OVRA agent, and we'll have to be on guard for his mischief. And, I'm sure he'll seek revenge many times over for what we did last night."

Sofia replied, "To rephrase the warning I offered last night, but now it's more inclusive: We'll watch each other's backs."

Without a flinch, Walter quipped, "Deal, Doctor *Signora* Sofia Savoy Russo." He finished his coffee, took her hand, and looked straight in her eyes. "Here's another deal. I'm here to help you, nothing more. Whatever we find, if anything, all the credit is yours. I have no need for recognition and I don't want it. If you ask, I'll help you write the report, but that'll be the end of it."

Sofia was taken aback by Walter's assertion. "Walter, that's not fair," she insisted. "We're equal team members. Credit for a find belongs to both of us, *capisci?*"

"*No comprender, signora.*" He rose from the table, put on his straw hat, and said, "The issue is settled. Let's shove off."

As they walked through the lobby, they spotted Segreti sitting in an overstuffed chair, pretending to read a newspaper. He acknowledged them with a forced, bitter, twisted smile.

Sofia's anger flared at the sight of him.

The pair climbed into the Auto Union Explorer and Sofia took the wheel. Shortly after they left the hotel and were several miles down a dirt road, Walter spotted a small Fiat automobile following them. Concerned, he asked Sofia, "Do you know about this Fiat that is following us?"

Nonplused, she responded, "It's that OVRA agent, Ugo Segreti, in his Fiat Topolino; it's the little one. He'll stick with us no matter what we do or where we go. We'll have to live with his intrusions. Now that you're with me, perhaps he'll moderate his abusive behavior."

They returned to the abandoned site from her last dig. Her two helpers were there, waiting. They had set up the tents, cut away the overgrown weeds, constructed a thorn-bush barricade around the camp to keep out small animals and perhaps some reptiles, and made the campsite as attractive and as livable as possible.

Sofia greeted her helpers, thanked them for setting up her camp so neatly, and introduced Walter. A few minutes later, Walter and Sofia entered her tent. She spread her annotated map of the area on her camp table, showed Walter the sites she'd previously explored for King Ezana's tomb, and explained the clues that prompted her decisions to dig at those sites. Walter remained quiet and attentive as he absorbed her information and correlated it with his knowledge of the area. She explained what clues she had remaining and pointed out the areas to which they pertained. Walter nodded in assent, as her reasoning fit neatly with his conclusions.

For the next seven days, Walter and Sofia worked from sunrise to sunset as an integrated team. They labored side by side with her two helpers, manning picks and shovels; it was some of the most intense manual labor Walter had done since his time on a drilling rig. With various sizes of screened and wood-framed trays, they shifted hundreds of pounds of dirt to find artifacts. Occasionally, they found a small ceramic or metal shard of no significance. But, evidence of King Ezana's tomb continued to evade them. The only positive outcome at the sites was that Segreti stayed out of their way. He sat on his camp stool, swigged his grappa, and lurked about occasionally, but mostly kept to himself. Nonetheless, they knew that he observed everything, and was accessing the scene with critical eyes and false judgments.

In the evenings, the utterly exhausted pair ate modest meals, discussed the day's results, and prepared for the next day's exploration.

Conversations were mostly limited to the necessary business of their dig. Occasionally, the camp experienced some excitement. One night, around midnight, a nearby lion's roars roused the camp to maximum alert. Her workers quickly reached their donkey and guarded it with their long, sharp spears. Only Segreti stepped outside with his weapon, the Beretta 38. All appreciated that the senior laborer had closed the camp's gateway with the thorn-bush barricade. After a few minutes, the roars began to fade and soon they ceased.

Another evening, shortly after dinner, a female Nubian ibex wandered into camp, walked to the trash pile for her next meal, and left without so much as a nod of thanks. Another day at the dig, a vixen and her two pups entered the site. She surveyed the scene and in a few minutes led her pups away to seek other business.

At sunrise on the eighth day, Sofia, with resignation in her voice, addressed Walter. "Let's delay our departure this morning. I'm tired. So far that King's tomb might as well be buried on Mars."

She sat on the running board of the Explorer, removed her bush hat, and slapped it on her knee. "Damn! I don't have any more options. My hands are blistered. My back aches. And I'm damn tired of that ignoble Ugo Segreti always watching us. Are we on a fool's errand, Walter? Is it time to conclude this venture, pack up and go home?"

Walter was not as frustrated as Sofia. He chose his words carefully. "Pardner, sure we haven't found anything. We're 'behind the curve', no doubt, and I've nothing more intellectually to contribute. But, I have plenty of muscle and resolve left, and it's ready for you to use. I also have fiscal resources, if you need them."

With haggard, soft brown eyes, Sofia looked up at Walter. "Thanks, my Texas protector." She leaned forward and put her head in her hands. Through her tears, she mumbled, "All this effort over so many years, my life's goal, so much energy and funds frittered away; the distress I've suffered is all for naught. Damn!" She stood up and wiped her eyes with her hands. "Walter, it's quits. I'm done. That damn king can stay buried. I don't care," she said with resolve.

Walter was somewhat disappointed, but compliant. He said, "Very well, Sofia. I reckon that you've made the right decision. But let's not break camp just yet. We'll head to our hotel and hold a serious powwow there."

Sofia felt better with Walter's unstinting support. "Deal, cowboy," she replied.

Sofia gave instructions to her helpers to keep the camp open. She would return tomorrow with her final decision. They climbed into the Explorer and headed toward Axum. Segreti's Fiat was close behind.

☙

Early that evening, the pair, each refreshed with a hot shower and a short nap under slow-moving overhead fans, and wearing fresh, comfort-able clothes, sat across from each other at a table near the garden window in the hotel's bar. Each sipped from a glass of pinot grigio. Segreti was at his usual position on a bar stool with a bottle of beer in his hand. From time to time, he glanced at the pair. Tonight the din from the chatting Italian officers and their demimondaines was not as severe as it had been.

Sofia had her map spread across the table. She and Walter worked diligently to fathom a strategy that might lead them to the tomb of King Ezana. However, now that they had only marginal or apocryphal information remaining, and considering their mental weariness, they tentatively decided to shut down their exploration activities for now. In a few days, they agreed, they would reassess their options.

Sofia folded her map and stored it in her field case. She took a deep drink of her wine and smiled broadly at Walter. Her brown eyes were now bright. She said casually, "Walter, I could not have gotten this far without you at my side and without your support. You've been my pillar of strength, and you've kept Segreti away from me. How can I thank you?"

Walter replied, *"No es nada, senora.* It's been my great pleasure to work with you, Sofia. As Tin Pan Alley meister Cole Porter penned, 'You're the top.' We're a great team." He paused before he said too much. "Since we're standing down for a few days, let's finish this wine and have a serious drink," he suggested.

Sofia grinned and said with sly good humor, "How serious, *signor*?" She leaned toward him and placed her head in the cup of her hands.

Walter had not seen Sofia so frivolous before. He liked it. Then it occurred to him that Sofia might be sending a more serious signal. He thought, *Maybe.* Then he rejected his thought as just imagination. "Let me introduce you to bourbon whiskey. It has a kick, so be cautious."

"I'll try most anything once." After a short pause, and with a mischievous smile, she cracked, "'Let's do it,' as your Mister Cole Porter suggests."

"That's a deal." Walter signaled the waiter, now a familiar fellow with great deference to the pair. "A bourbon for the lady over several pieces of ice, and I'll have a double straight up."

Two rounds later, both were pleasantly tipsy. Sofia finished her drink and put her glass down a little too hard. "Walter, you've hooked me with this bourbon whiskey. It's wonderful! What will I do when I'm with my friends in Rome? They'll be shocked at my un-Italian behavior, drinking Kentucky whiskey."

Walter smiled faintly and replied, "With your character and fortitude, I'm sure you'll convert those folks to your rash ways. I reckon we ought to order something to eat. It's getting late. What'll you have?"

"Not yet, Walter. Come sit next to me. I've something to tell you. It's private, and it's imperative that Segreti doesn't overhear. *Capisci?*"

Walter's senses went on high alert. He stood and took Sofia's hand. "We're going for a walk in the garden. There are too many ears about. Stay here. I'll be right back."

He went to Segreti and said, "Sofia and I are going for a walk in the garden. We'll stay near the window so you can keep track of us."

Segreti did not respond; he turned away and ordered another beer.

A few minutes into their walk, Sofia said, "Thanks again, Walter. Going outside was the right move."

Walter took hold of her hand and they continued walking. The bourbon had boosted Sofia's courage and she knew to the depth of her soul that she could trust Walter implicitly. "Walter, what I'm about to tell you is my secret. Can I trust you?"

"Whatever happens, Sofia, I'll never betray you," he equivocated. "What's on your mind?"

"Actually, there is more to my expedition than the search for King Ezana's tomb." She paused to ensure that her next words were accurate and complete. "Late in my last expedition to this area, I stumbled on a hidden cave that was outside my OVRA control zone. Inside, I found some very old artifacts that will have major archeological import regarding the history of this area. Luckily, Ugo Segreti was drunk and did not realize that I was away." As they continued walking, she revealed the circumstances of how she stumbled on the cave and the details of what she found. "Unfortunately, I did not have time to explore the cave further. I'll need help with this find. Can I count on you?"

"That's an amazing story," Walter replied. "Yes, of course, I'll help you. Again, I won't lay any claims to your discovery. What's your plan?"

"Let's leave early tomorrow morning. We'll spend the day taking inventory of the artifacts, and photographing them with my Leica. Our major obstacle is Ugo Segreti. We've got to prevent him from following us. If we are not successful in losing him, we'll be in serious trouble. He'll report that we are missing and the OVRA will expend maximum effort to find and arrest us. I shiver to think of being in an OVRA prison. I wouldn't be able to stand the torture and interrogations. I'd die."

"Maybe not. I'll see if I can disable the Fiat without arousing his suspicions. How far is this cave from our current site?"

"Not far, perhaps three or four miles. We'll have to hike to it."

"I'll work the Segreti problem and get it done this evening. Be ready to travel at dawn." He took her back inside the hotel and escorted her to the stairs. "Goodnight, Sofia." He kissed her hand, mimicking what he had seen Europeans do in the movies.

"One of these days you're going to do better than that, Mister Gregory."

Walter went to Segreti, who was now palpably drunk. "Segreti, be alert and listen to me. The *signora* and I are leaving the hotel at dawn tomorrow to go to our dig."

☙

Around midnight, the lobby was deserted, the bar closed, and Joseph, who never seemed to sleep, was at his post at the desk.

Walter approached the desk. "Joseph, I need a quart of water and a funnel."

"Of course, Mister Gregory. May I be so bold as to ask to what purpose you need such equipment?"

"That you may, Joseph. That you may. You've been a stellar undercover contact. I'm going to sabotage Ugo Segreti's Fiat."

Joseph said, "May I suggest that *we* are going to disable that Fiat. I'll get the equipment and meet you at the automobile."

Joseph caught Walter off guard with his "we," and his insistence that he was going to help. "Joseph, I can handle this alone. Stay and keep manning this desk. I don't want you compromised."

"Mister Gregory, I'll explain at the Fiat."

Ten minutes later, the pair was in the hotel's parking lot at the Fiat. Joseph was holding the funnel and Walter was pouring the water, being careful not to spill any. When the task was completed, they walked back to the hotel lobby. "Okay, Joseph, fess up. What's going on?"

With a touch of contrition in his voice, Joseph confessed, "I'm afraid that I've not been totally honest with you, Mister Gregory.

It's true that I am a freelance undercover agent working for your State Department's Bureau of Intelligence and Research. But, in my real life, I am a bona fide agent for the British MI6. My controller directed me to render all possible aid to you—no matter what."

Caught off guard, Walter's mind raced to comprehend fully the impact of Joseph's announcement. He smiled broadly and said, "Joseph, you are a scallywag. I missed all the clues because I was too focused on my assignment." Walter leaned on the counter and tapped his fingers on it. "I should have known that there was a sub rosa context to this *soirée*. Rodriquez tipped his hand when he told me that there was a British destroyer standing by in the Red Sea to evacuate me. But, I missed the connection. That's what I get for being an amateur."

"It is of no importance, Mister Gregory. What counts are results."

"One last item to consider, Joseph. Tomorrow, Ugo Segreti is going to be hopping mad when his automobile stalls several miles down the road and he can't follow *Signora* Russo and me. He'll soon know it was sabotage. Can you concoct a scenario that will placate him, and throw off suspicion that the *Signora* or I were involved?"

"Of course. I was anticipating you taking such an action." Joseph smiled broadly. "I'll take care of it shortly after you retire."

Walter climbed the stairs to his suite and concluded that Joseph had keen "thinking room" between those dark eyes of his.

After Walter had retired, Joseph returned to the parking lot and vandalized several other automobiles he knew belonged to Italian officers.

chapter ten

En route to the Hidden Cave near Axum, Abyssinia.
4 September 1937.

he next morning, Walter and Sofia left the hotel as scheduled and drove away in the Auto Union Explorer. Within a few minutes, Walter spotted Ugo Segreti's Fiat close behind. "Care to place a small bet on when that Fiat conks out?" he said with an elfish grin.

"No deal, *amico mio.*" She peeked in the rearview mirror and saw the Fiat dropping back. "Looks as if your mischief is working. He's falling behind."

Segreti's automobile's engine began to cough and the vehicle jerked about as the water entered the carburetor and starved the engine of gasoline. In a few seconds, the engine quit. With his stalled Fiat on the side of the dirt road, Segreti was stranded several miles from the hotel and had no immediate prospect of either repairing his automobile or quickly getting other transportation to follow the escaping pair. His anger at being duped overwhelmed him. He sat on the running board as the adrenaline retreated, and he planned stinging revenge on the perpetrator—suspecting that Walter Gregory was the culprit.

Walter glanced back at the stalled Fiat and commented, "He's done. And we're free of him. Let's move out."

After a couple of hours, they arrived at their current dig. Sofia told her crew to stay there and clean the camp. "I should return before nightfall." Walter and she packed their knapsacks with high-protein food, tools, scaling rope, and potable water. After double-checking their equipment, they started their hike to the cave.

About the same time, Ugo Segreti, disheveled and puffing, stormed into the lobby of the Goha Hotel and charged the desk. With his eyes icy cold, he snapped, "My automobile has been sabotaged. Sabotaged, do you hear? It was that damn Texan, Gregory, I'm sure of it." With a sardonic scowl he asserted, "Those blackguards have eluded me—a representative of the OVRA—to go where, no one knows. They'll pay dearly for this." He wiped his brow with his hand-kerchief. "Give me the telephone, I must call OVRA headquarters."

Joseph saw a tired, disillusioned fellow trying too hard to com-plete his assignment while not having the wherewithal to accomplish it. With a sincere voice, he responded with faux empathy. "Mister Segreti, I am so sorry for your distress. I hope your Fiat isn't beyond repair. If I may, let me suggest that the damage to your automobile probably wasn't the result of Mister Gregory's activities."

Before Joseph could continue, Segreti interrupted, "How can you suggest such nonsense? He and that Italian trollop of his are responsible. I know it. They've been trying to elude me for days," he exaggerated.

Segreti's derogatory words about Doctor *Signora* Sofia Russo stung Joseph deeply and solidified his resolve to have his revenge on this Italian oaf. Nonetheless, he responded quietly, "Mister Segreti, last evening, sometime around midnight, a group of unruly youth invaded our parking lot and vandalized several automobiles belonging to our very important Italian guests. Yours must have been included in their shenanigans. Several of our staff and I rushed to the parking lot and shooed them away." He picked up the counter telephone and asked, "Should I dial OVRA headquarters for you?"

Segreti, somewhat calmer, realized that if he reported that he'd lost track of Doctor Russo, he'd be in serious trouble. "On reflection, that's not necessary. Call a garage and have their wrecker tow my automobile to their facility and repair it. Tell them I'll need it by this evening."

❧

The temperature was a moderate seventy-two degrees in the high plain, alpine area northwest of Axum, and the sounds of the bush penetrated the scene. Sofia and Walter had been hiking for about an hour. The narrow and twisted trail followed the rim of the Tekeze River—all too familiar to Sofia. Walter noted that Sofia moved with resolute energy and enduring self-confidence. In several places, the river pooled and, without exception, crocodiles were present. All too often, flash floods from the river had washed away the trail, causing Walter and Sofia to detour deep into the bush. Whenever they had to leave the trail, the pair went on high alert for dangerous animals, venomous reptiles, and sinkholes that often were covered with vegetation—some of the sinkholes could be as deep as ten feet.

Sofia looked about the area and spoke. "Walter, we're now clearly outside my OVRA-designated travel zone. The authorities have closed all of the surrounding area to any civilian entry. If we're spotted, we'll be in serious trouble and probably arrested." She continued hiking for a few steps. "Walter, are you game to continue?"

"Of course," he said with strong conviction. "I'm committed."

"Thanks, Texas. I wouldn't be successful without your support. Today is my last chance to explore that cave and its artifacts. It's now or never."

"We'll make it." Walter picked up the pace slightly as they got closer to the cave. He looked compassionately at Sofia and took her hand. His guilt began to rise slowly as he approached the goal of his assignment. His mind raced: *I've been dishonest with this indefatigable and warmhearted woman.* He had betrayed her trust by his silence and dissembling about his secret motives. Albeit he'd helped and befriended her, he had used her selfishly. In a few more steps he acknowledged, *I'm not her friend, she is much more than that. I care for her deeply. Is it love? Don't know. Never been there. Whatever it is, I like it and want more."*

"Heads up, Walter!" Sofia shouted and grabbed his arm.

Walter snapped back to reality and saw the large gap in the trail that he had been about to step into. He stepped backwards, then smiled without humor. "Wow! Many thanks, my Italian sherpa. I'm in your debt."

"That you are, Texas cowboy, and I intend to collect." Sofia smiled with sly good humor.

Walter took Sofia's hand again as they began to move into a section of very thick brush. Walter drew his six-shooter as they cautiously advanced. Their detour was much longer and deeper into the bush than the others had been. About five minutes later, Sofia stumbled over a metal container. Walter caught her before she hit the ground. Recovered, she pointed to the object and barked, "What the devil is that? And what's it doing in this last end of civilization?"

Walter used his machete to cut away brush surrounding this object. He knelt to inspect it, but could not see it clearly because of the vines that covered most of it. He asked Sofia, "Please grab my flashlight and shine it on this thing."

In a few minutes, he had the object exposed enough to see clearly that it was a narrow, metal, gas canister about two feet long. Immediately, he knew what it was. "My God!" He shouted, "Sofia, get the hell away from here. Move! Now! No questions. Get out!"

Intensely startled, Sofia reeled backward a few steps. Never in her life had she been commanded to action in such a boisterous manner. Nonetheless, she dropped the flashlight, and lurched into the thick brush back to the trail, scratching her arms and ripping tears in her trousers. "Walter, what's happening?" she shouted. "For God's sake, tell me what you've found."

Walter didn't respond. He was intently focused on this thing. He retrieved the flashlight, brushed aside some remaining dirt, and shined the light on the lettering. Immediately, staring at him was a large, flaming-red skull and crossbones symbol ensconced in a diamond-like polygon. Just below, he recognized the words "*FOSGENE*" and "*PERICOLO*." On the cylinder's side, he could see "*Regia Aeronautica Italiana*."

Sofia waited anxiously. *What had Walter found? And if it's so damn dangerous, why doesn't he get out of there?* Impatient for a response, she shouted, "Walter, what's happening? What are you doing?" She waited impatiently for a prompt answer. But he did not respond. "Damn you, Walter Gregory, I'm coming in there after you. *Capisci?*"

"No! Stay back. I'll join you in a few minutes." He carefully lifted the cylinder off the ground, and saw that the top valve had been blown off—undoubtedly by the fuse mechanism. It was empty. Dropped by an Italian aircraft, its poison gas must have terrorized and murdered innocent people. The empty cylinder weighed about two pounds. "I'm coming out now, Sofia. Stay there."

Walter carried the canister to where Sofia was waiting. She glanced at the canister and before he could speak, she chided him with a sudden urgency, "Walter Gregory Texas I ought to smack you! You scared me!" Calming rapidly, she smiled. "Thanks for the warning, pal."

Walter, properly chastised, replied, "My apologies." With feverish energy in his voice, he continued. "I had to act quickly to get you out of the area. I had suspicions about what this thing is, but I wasn't sure it was a dud." He showed her the cylinder and pointed to the symbol and inscriptions. "Sofia, this thing is a phosgene canister. Here's proof that the fascists poisoned Abyssinians in their last campaign. It contained that deadly gas under high pressure, and when it hit the ground, the impact initiated a fuse that blew open the sealed cap, and it spewed the gas in all directions as it spun around and around. This weapon kills without discrimination or mercy."

"*Mio Dio*," Sofia exclaimed. "It's inhuman. Monstrous murders! I had no idea that General Graziani was so ruthless—he's a long-time family friend." She paused, placed her hand on the canister, and moved it up and down over the death symbol. "Rather, I should say, he was such a friend."

"General Graziani must have had direct orders from Mussolini to authorize such a dastardly act of war." Walter shook his head and said, "In this nutty world, government bureaucrats have devised a set of rules on how armies may kill each other. The League of Nations Geneva Protocol bans the use of poison gas. It's genocide." Walter rolled the canister into his hands for a close inspection. Walter continued with emphasis, "My dear Sofia, this phosgene canister explains with crystal clarity why the OVRA required you to keep out of this area. The rogues didn't complete their cleanup. We've found the proverbial 'smoking gun.' This phosgene canister explicitly confirms the rumors that the fascists used poison gas on the Abyssinians, and we're going to expose those fascists to the civilized world."

Sofia reacted with an anger that was mixed with disbelief, disillusionment, and resentment. "I'm heartbroken and deeply embarrassed at what my countrymen have done." She wiped a tear with her handkerchief. "Of course, I'm with you," she said with a certain poised dignity.

"Deal, Sofia. Let's see what else we can find." The pair began to search the brush. Soon Walter cried out, "Here's another one."

Sofia spotted several others. "There are more canisters over here."

"Let's see that map of yours."

The pair saw that they were close to the village of Hawzēr, about two thousand feet ahead. "Come on, Sofia. I want to see that place." A few minutes later, they entered what was left of Hawzēr. It was peacefully quiet—not a soul was about, and the still-standing huts were abandoned. Inside several, they saw evidence that the residents evacuated hurriedly—or were poisoned where they were.

"I can't stand this anymore.," Sofia whispered hoarsely.

"Sofia, snap some photographs of this place and those canisters you spotted over there."

Within ten minutes, Sofia had completed her photography. They loaded the canisters in their backpacks—two in his and one in hers.

Walter urged, "We have enough evidence. Let's get out of here."

Racing through their minds was the surety that if the OVRA discovered that they had these phosgene canisters, they would be arrested and executed.

Walter took Sofia's hand and they began to hike to the trail.

chapter eleven

Along the Tekeze River, Abyssinia. 4 September 1937.

With the phosgene canisters stored securely in their backpacks, Walter and Sofia continued their hike on the narrow trail along the Tekeze River as it raged between gaps in the mountains. At one spot, the trail evaporated and the pair had to struggle to move forward. "Damn," Sofia spouted. "This river has been on a rampage since I was here last spring."

Some time later, they entered a flat area and Walter called a halt. "It's time to rest and evaluate our situation." He and Sofia removed their backpacks, took deep drinks of water, and munched on dried fruit, hardtack, and jerky. "Where do you reckon we are? And what's your estimate for how much farther it is to this cave?" Walter quizzed.

"I'm not lost. I'm just not sure where I am," Sofia quipped. She cracked a thin, mocking smile. She stood and looked carefully at their surroundings. "The trail, what there is of it, is so different. But the overall landscape is familiar. I sense that we are close. If I can spot the waterfall that swept me into the pool, we'll be there."

Walter rose and hoisted on his backpack. "Okay, let's keep moving. We'll press on for an hour. Deal?"

"Deal."

For the next thirty minutes, the pair struggled for each step forward. As a safety precaution, they tied a belaying rope between them. A fall into the cold, turbulent river could be fatal.

"There it is! There!" cried Sofia as they entered a large meadow. Ahead were the waterfall and the large pool that had been instrumental in saving Sofia's life last spring. The trail was clear and firm. The bank was steeply inclined and the pool was about fifteen feet below the trail. She unhooked the rope and moved smartly forward, looking for the rock marker she'd left. "Damn! It's not here. The rock marker I made is gone."

Walter caught up and assured her, "That's okay, Sofia. Before we do anything, let's see if we spot any crocodiles in that pool." The pair searched around the shoreline and did not see any of the dangerous reptiles. Walter suggested, "Even though we don't see any, doesn't mean there aren't any. They could be under the water."

"Not likely. On this balmy day, I suspect that they'd be sunning on the shore."

"Okay, let's find that cave."

They scoured the bank, looking down for indications of the opening. A few minutes later, Sofia exclaimed in frustration, "Nothing. I don't see anything familiar on that slope."

"That's okay, pardner. We'll find it." He tossed off his backpack and sat in the soft grass. Let's attack this problem with our wits. It has to be nearby."

"Yes, indeed." Sofia sat next to him. "What's on your mind?"

He took a swig from his canteen and passed it to Sofia. "No serious germs on this thing."

She drank heartily, which eased her anxiety.

"Here's the deal. We're going to that waterfall to refresh your memory." He urged her to recount, as best she could, the exact sequence of events leading up to her discovery of the cave.

A few minutes later, Walter said, "That's great. The opening should be about twenty feet from the base of the falls and perhaps about ten feet up from the pool." He walked off seven paces. "Let's start our search here."

They rigged a rope to a tree and Walter repelled down the steeply inclined bank, which was thickly covered with underbrush. He used a stout tree limb to tap the bank in the areas he couldn't reach. Nothing. There was only solid bank. Over the next hour, they worked this process repeatedly: each time, Walter moved his search several feet toward the falls. Still nothing.

"Time out, Sofia," Walter shouted. He climbed to the rim of the bank and collapsed, spread-eagled on the grass.

Sofia sat beside him, and rubbed his neck. "Have faith, Walter, I know we are close."

Soon he sat up and drank deeply from his canteen. "I'm ready. This time we'll work away from the falls."

On his third try in that direction, while Sofia was manning the ropes, she heard a ringing, "Eureka! It's here." Sofia tied off the ropes and looked over at the grinning Walter.

"Pardner, it's right here." He used his machete to clear the underbrush away from the opening. "Send down our backpacks and come down."

An exultant Sofia snapped a salute and replied, "As you say, sir."

Walter put their backpacks on the small ledge in front of the cave's opening, and told Sofia to rappel down. Walter grabbed her waist and held her close to him, perhaps a little too long.

Sofia, delightfully pleased, teased him with, "Kind sir, unhand this fair maiden, who is only slightly soiled." She turned around and kissed him on the cheek. "That's just the teaser—more later."

Before they entered the cave, Walter said, "Let's leave our backpacks here at the entrance on this narrow shelf. No need to lug all that equipment inside. We'll take in only what we'll need. He also suggested that they cover their mouths and noses with their bandannas.

As he began these tasks, Sofia, with a puzzled look, asked, "What's up?"

"A safety precaution. No telling what the musty air in there might contain. Frequently, abandoned caves like this one are contaminated with a fungus called Valley Fever—a lung infection that can cause serious problems."

"That's new information. Okay." Sofia tied off her bandanna.

With flashlights on, they entered the cave and carefully moved deeper into it. Walter said with a touch of caution, "Sofia, walk softly and try to minimize kicking up the dust. The fungi could be anywhere."

In a few short steps, Sofia commented that nothing remained of the reptile she had killed. But the expended brass littered the area.

Walter offered, "Probably some scavenger carried the carcass away. And that brass tells us that no one has been here." As they moved, he noticed in the flashlight beam the fine dust being scattered. Several dozen steps ahead, their light caught one of the amphorae.

"Walter, here they are!" she exclaimed. "*Grazie, a dio!*" Within a few feet, the pair was at the edge of the artifact perimeter.

"Sofia, if I may suggest, take your photographs now, before we disturb this area," Walter said with marked emphasis.

"I agree." In the next few minutes Sofia, moving carefully among the artifacts, used her Leica camera with the flashbulb reflector attached. On each artifact, she carefully focused the lens, calculated and set the f-stop, and pushed the trigger; a brilliant light filled the cave as the flashbulb exploded. She snapped a complete roll of thirty-six black and white negatives. Some shots were tight close-ups of the lettering on the shards. Finished, she stored her camera and moved to pick up one of the intact amphora.

Walter grabbed her and pulled her away smartly. "No, Sofia! Stay away from those things."

Slightly miffed at Walter's harsh treatment and perplexed by his peculiar command, Sofia demanded, "What the hell is going on, Walter Gregory? You're acting like a madman. What's the matter with you? Tell me now!"

Walter saw the fury in her eyes and realized that he could no longer deceive her. "Very well. I'll meet you at the entrance." His forehead was wet with nervous perspiration. "I'll join you in a few minutes. I've some work to do."

"What work, Walter?" This time her voice was tinged with uncertainty and fear.

He did not respond or look at her. Rather, he used his small pick and spade and took rock samples from locations throughout the cave and stored them in a lead-foil-lined leather pouch.

Sofia watched him, dumbfounded. Her eyes widened in disbelief. As she glared at him, her lips moved in a near soundless whisper, "What are you doing? Answer me."

His task completed, Walter took Sofia's arm and led her to the entrance. Despondent and with a tinge of regret, he said, "My dear Sofia, the dust on those artifacts is contaminated with dangerously high radioactivity. I had to stop you from touching anything. My scenario regarding Valley Fever was a ruse to prevent us from breathing that radioactive dust."

Sofia blinked a couple of times at this staggering information. She drew several steadying breaths, and demanded in a hard, hoarse voice, "Walter, the truth. All of it. Now!"

"Yes, of course." He paused to bolster his courage. "The bottom line is that I am an American agent on assignment for our State Department's Bureau of Intelligence and Research. My task is to get samples of the ore in this cave and smuggle it out so that our scientists can evaluate it for reasons that must be kept secret." His face was grim; his eyes narrowed. "Through clandestine sources, we knew of your activities in Abyssinia and Cairo, and arranged for you to get the visa to return here."

At first, Sofia was flabbergasted at Walter's explication. Then, bitter anger overwhelmed her. Hate flared in her eyes. "Damn you, Walter Gregory, you betrayed me! You don't care for me! You stole my affection under a perfidious false flag. You used me as one of your gullible flappers, to be tossed aside when through."

She wanted to sob, but held her composure. She could not contain her fury. She wound up a right-handed haymaker and walloped Walter squarely on the tip of his chin. He was sent reeling against the side of the cave and slipped to the floor, stirring clouds of dust that engulfed both of them. "You unholy *bastardo,* I ought to kill you." She drew and pointed her Beretta 32 at Walter's heart. She tried to squeeze the trigger but her index finger would not function. Searing pain raced through her right hand. She saw it was becoming swollen and brightly discolored. *Damn, I broke my finger.* With her left hand, she grabbed her damaged hand, slid to the floor, stirring up more dust, ducked her head between her knees, and bawled plaintively.

Walter rubbed his bruised chin, recovered his wits, sat next to Sofia, held her in his arms and let her sob. Within a few minutes, he said, "Sofia, please get up. We have to get out of here."

Without comment, she rose. They exited the cave and stood on the small ledge. He took her right hand and assessed the damage, "When we're on top of the bank, I'll work on your hand." He evaluated their options. "I'm going up top and then I'll haul you up. Help as much as you can." Within a few minutes, both were on the top of the bank with their backpacks.

Walter took Sofia's right hand and saw the swelling and discoloration. "This will hurt." He slowly and gently moved her damaged finger back and forth.

Sofia emitted a small cry of pain. "Walter, you certainly know how to torture a woman. What do you conclude?"

"It's probably not broken, but you've damaged some ligaments." He retrieved two wooden spoons from his kit, trimmed them to make a splint, and wrapped her finger in gauze. "That'll do it until we return to Axum."

"Thanks, Walter."

He took her in his arms and held her affectionately. "My dear Sofia, please accept my apology for deceiving and using you. My assignment is of great national importance for my country—and all democracies." He paused to form his next comment precisely. "Although I was inherently dishonest with you, in no way is my affection for you false. You are a treasure that I hold dear."

Sofia pulled away slightly away from his arms, forced a small smile, and said, "Walter, I do not understand your explanation, but I accept your contrition." She wiped away her tears. "Thanks for taking care of my finger. And I apologize for my eruption and threatening you with my Beretta. Thank God I could not pull the trigger."

"I could see in your eyes you meant to. We're still a team, right?"

"Partners," she quipped. "Walter, what are we to do about the amphora and parchments in the cave? That's why I am here; to inventory and bring them out to be studied by experts."

"Not now, Sofia. After the war, which we know is on the horizon, we'll mount a proper expedition to retrieve them with scientific precision and with permission of the government. For now, we leave them alone."

Disappointed, Sofia had to accept the inevitability of Walter's logic. "So be it."

Walter knew with absolute certainty that they had to wash away the radioactive dust on their clothes and in their hair. He stood and walked on the high bank toward the far end of the pool. About five hundred feet ahead, he spotted a bright, sandy beach and saw that the river's bank sloped gently toward it. He took Sofia's left arm to help her stand. "Sofia, we've got to get this radioactive dust off us. There's a beach ahead with easy access to the pool. Let's go."

At the shore, he checked for crocodiles, saw none, and plunged into the refreshing water. He ducked under several times. "Come in, Sofia, the water's fine."

Now fully recovered, she plunged into the pool and emitted a small cry of pleasure. She too splashed about and ducked under to rid herself of the dust.

Walter, now lying on the beach to let the sun dry his clothes, called out, "Having a fine time, *Signora?*"

With a hint of devilment she responded, "Indeed, I am." She rushed to the shore, kicking off her clothes. "Walter Gregory, you're too hard to dismiss."

They satiated their passions.

chapter twelve

Goha Hotel, Axum, Abyssinia. 4 September 1937.

It was late when Sofia and Walter returned to the hotel. Although extremely tired and dirty, they were fulfilled: they had found the cave and the artifacts were undisturbed; they had three Italian phosgene canisters; and Sofia's seduction of Walter had ended the foreplay banter.

Walter stopped at the desk and whispered to the indefatigable Joseph, "Notify your controller, we are leaving tomorrow."

"Very well."

Walter took Sofia's arm and said, "Sofia, the film in your Leica has undeveloped images of the amphora and inscriptions, the Hawzâr village, and the phosgene canisters. That's critically important information. We don't want to lose it."

Puzzled, she cocked her head slightly. "I do not understand why we would lose my film. It is secured firmly in my camera, in the backpack."

"Exactly. That film was exposed to enough radiation to fog it severely over time. It's got to be developed soon."

With a sly smile, Sofia responded, "Makes sense, Texan." She whispered to Joseph, "I have a roll of black and white film that must be developed—away from OVRA's prying eyes. Any ideas?"

With a slight eagerness in his voice, Joseph responded, "Indeed, *Signora*, I know of a darkroom nearby." He smiled with wily cocksureness. "Not long ago, some associates of mine had one installed in the back of the laundry room in the basement."

Sofia dug the Leica out of her backpack, handed it to Joseph, and said, "No prints. Just the negatives in a preserver sleeve."

"Very well. I will have them for you shortly."

"Thank you, Joseph."

Sofia perused the hotel lobby and bar, looking for Segreti, but did not see him. "Joseph, have you seen our OVRA agent?"

With a guilty smile, he said proudly, "No *Signora*. I've not seen *Signore* Segreti since early this morning, when he was in an awful state. Someone had sabotaged his automobile, and he was not able to escort you to your dig. I imagine that his absence stressed you mightily. Is that not so, *Signora* Russo?"

A smile spread across Sofia's face and she teased, "Joseph, please understand that I was devastated. I worried the entire day, wondering when his presence would grace my dig."

Joseph noticed the splint on Sofia's finger. "May I see your damaged finger? Is it broken?"

"No. I had an accident and Mister Gregory managed this temporary splint."

"Is it painful?"

"Yes."

"May I see your finger? I've had some medical training."

"You have medical training?"

"Yes. Of course." Joseph realized that he had made a faux pas. He continued rather too quickly, "It is part of my job here at the hotel."

Her skeptical antennae became attuned; she'd never heard Joseph mention medical training, and she couldn't imagine that it was part of his job as a desk clerk.

"Joseph, you interest me. May I ask, where did you get your medical training?"

Walter interceded. "Sofia, let's get to the bar. I'm thirsty. We'll attend to your finger later. A couple swigs of bourbon are all the pain reliever you need for now."

"Walter, I need straightforward answers, and my finger hurts. "Perhaps Joseph can relieve my pain and anxiety. Where, Joseph?"

"*Signora*, my training was here and there." He repeated awkwardly. "Here and there. No place in particular."

With questioning eyes, she said, "Thank you, Joseph." She extended her right hand to him. Some past events were crystallizing into a coherent pattern. She had observed that Joseph and Walter had been too friendly, considering the social gap between them. And, Joseph was always nearby when they were in the lobby, bar, or restaurant. She concluded that Joseph was probably not what he seemed to be. *But what?* Her imagination ran wild with improbable scenarios. Nonetheless, she was convinced that Walter and Joseph were in cahoots and were engaged in some sort of skullduggery. She'd find out soon enough.

Joseph undid the bandages, removed the make-do splints, inspected the sprained finger, and commented, "It doesn't appear to be broken; just swollen due to trauma. May I work on your finger, *Signora*?"

"Yes, Joseph. Please do."

Joseph removed small wooden splints from his first-aid kit, trimmed them to size, placed them on her finger, and wrapped it with fresh gauze.

She squirmed as a stabbing pain shot through her finger.

Noticing the bruise on Walter's chin, Joseph commented slyly, "That should do it, *Signora* Russo. Try not to hit anything with your hand. The swelling and coloring should begin to fade in a few days."

"Thank you, Joseph. You are very clever," she answered in a tired voice.

The pair stopped at the hotel bar; Sofia ordered a glass of Chianti, Walter bourbon on ice. They talked quietly about their day's adventures, skipping the unpleasant episode, and not dwelling on their intimacy. They tried to maintain a demeanor of normalcy, though they were fearful that the OVRA would discover that they had the damning canisters.

Ugo Segreti stormed into the bar, spotted Sofia and Walter, and rushed headlong to their table. An angry distortion deformed one corner of his mouth. He demanded, "Where have you been, *Signora* Sofia Savoy Russo?"

Sofia replied cattily, "Why are you angry with me, *Signore* Segreti? What have I done?"

"You deceived me. You violated your parole by evading my escort." His face was flushed an angry brick red. "I shall report your misadventures to *Colonnello* Jacopo Visco at OVRA headquarters, and he will arrest you and your paramour."

"*Signore* Segreti, please understand, I was at my dig today."

"Not true, Russo. I was there and your workers said you and this fellow drove off to the northwest. You know that is a restricted area and I must accompany you on any travels."

Realizing that she was in serious trouble, Sofia softened her harsh rhetoric. "*Signore* Segreti, you have exaggerated what happened today. We saw you following us in your Fiat and then falling back, and we concluded that you would catch up shortly." She added, with more sincerity in her voice, "We were at my dig today and reckoned that to continue searching there was fruitless." Deeply anxious, she took a deep breath and with sincere eyes, she continued. "Mister Gregory and I spent the day exploring a couple of areas to the northwest of my current dig, and I'm convinced that we stayed out of the OVRA restricted zone. We found a few sparse clues to King Ezana's tomb and will explore them further," she lied.

His lips moved soundlessly and with a sardonic scowl, he moved to a nearby table and ordered a mug of beer. He frequently looked up and stared at Sofia.

The pair sipped their drinks quietly as their anxiety built over Segreti's threat to report Sofia to OVRA headquarters. When they did speak, it was innocuous badinage. The bar area was especially warm this evening, and Sofia took off her field jacket. Carelessly, she had failed to button her blouse completely after her tryst on the beach.

Sofia saw that Segreti was staring at her lasciviously, and she realized that her blouse was not covering her brassiere.

Segreti continued to stare at her sensual, rounded breast.

"Damn that Segreti, he's a lecher."

Walter said, "Ignore him. We are in deep enough trouble, don't compound our problem." He ordered another round.

Sofia cracked, "Order double bourbon for me." She sipped her whiskey as Segreti continued to stare at her. Unbridled, she downed the remaining bourbon in one gulp as anger flashed in her eyes. She ignored prudence, jumped up impulsively, and marched to his table. Her eyes smoldered with hate and her mouth was pursed tightly. "Agent Ugo Segreti of the OVRA, come and join Walter and me. It will be so much easier for you to have a clearer view of my bosom and to eavesdrop on us," she sniped.

He looked at her and saw the rage in her face. "No, thank you, *Signora* Russo. I am more comfortable here. I intend to retire shortly."

Joseph observed the confrontation from his post and knew a climax to this scenario was imminent.

A calmer Sofia returned to the table and ordered another round. "Walter, I am so sorry. That was a stupid performance." There was fear in her eyes and fear in her hollow-sounding voice. After yet another round, they ordered a simple dinner, and then they called it quits for the day. They picked up their backpacks and went to their suites to shower and rest.

At Sofia's door, Walter said, "Tomorrow morning we will plan how to cope with the OVRA." He did not reveal to her that he had made plans for them to escape the next day. He kissed her quickly and entered his suite next door.

Just as Sofia was about to enter her suite, the ubiquitous Joseph approached and said, "*Signora,* here is that information." He handed her a standard business envelope. "The news is excellent, I might add."

She took the envelope, and tucked it in a jacket pocket. "*Grazie,* Joseph."

Sofia's body ached and she was bone tired. She undressed and put on her robe. She paced the floor, thinking about the day's events. Anxiety gripped her. She slipped the Beretta 32 into the robe's pocket. Its slight heft and its promise of some security stirred her courage. She decided a bath would help ease her concerns.

As Sofia bathed, she thought about her desperate situation and suddenly felt a surge of panic. If the OVRA arrested her, it would end her career and terminate her archeological research. The secret police would harass her extended family in Rome. On reflection, she gasped at the realization that the OVRA probably would rape and torture her, then let her die in agony. A news release would note that a wild animal had attacked her. No matter what happened, Walter would be engulfed in her troubles. Each day, Segreti had become bolder, increasingly obnoxious, more lecherous, and more threatening. He made it clear that he had power over her. She stepped out of the tub and began to shake with fear. She needed Walter. She threw on her robe and dashed next door. She was almost hysterical when he took her in his arms to comfort her. His strong arms and soothing words soon calmed her. Shortly they were on his bed as one.

೧

Segreti was now committed to turning Sofia over to the OVRA, but he wanted some marginally believable evidence of her anti-fascist activities to make his charges foolproof. He followed the pair upstairs, hid in a cleaning closet, and peeked through a crack in the door. He watched as Sofia left her room and entered Walter's.

In her haste, Sofia had left her door unlocked. Segreti left his hiding place, went to her door, tried the knob, and entered her room. He began searching for evidence. He rifled through her backpack, tossing its contents about. At the bottom, he found the phosgene canister. Shocked, yet eminently pleased, he let out a silent cry of success. As he was about to leave, his prurient proclivities kicked in as he heard, through the paper-thin walls, the pair expending their passion. He climbed on her bed and put his head next to the wall to hear more clearly.

Joseph had shadowed Segreti. A few minutes after the OVRA agent entered Sofia's suite, Joseph flung the door open and confronted him with his British-issued Enfield 38 caliber revolver. With surprising speed, Segreti knocked Joseph's gun to the floor. A scuffle ensued and the diminutive Joseph was no match for the heavy Segreti. In a few seconds, Segreti had damaged Joseph so severely that he was on the floor, bleeding, and barely conscious. "You stupid MI6 agent. Did you not realize that I knew of your connection to British intelligence?" With deadly aim, Segreti shot Joseph between the eyes.

The noise of the shot penetrated Walter's suite. "It's from your room, Sofia." With sudden clarity, both instinctively surmised that Segreti was involved. Horrified, Sofia realized that she had left her backpack in her room. She concluded Segreti had probably found the canister, and shot someone who interrupted him.

Sofia and Walter threw on their robes and dashed into her suite. She entered first and drew her Beretta 32 from the pocket of her robe. Segreti was bending over the dead Joseph, searching his clothing. The canister was under his arm. Her possessions were scattered. Her eyes smoldered with hate and the madness of fear, and she instinctively fired her weapon several times, hitting the OVRA agent in the abdomen.

Badly wounded, Segreti collapsed to the floor and grabbed his mid-section with both hands as blood oozed between his fingers. He stared at Sofia with wrath smoldering in his eyes. He tried to raise his pistol, but Sofia kicked it away. Sofia had no remorse or anxiety; she moved close to the fallen OVRA agent and aimed her pistol at his head for the *coup de grâce*.

Walter restrained her. "That's enough, Sofia. Let him die in agony. We're in enough trouble." He went to Joseph, and shook his head. "He was a good man. When we're out of this country and safely in Allied hands, I'll write a comprehensive report for his controller."

Sofia asked, "FBI, French ANSSI, MI6, or what?"

"MI6."

Her adrenaline subsided, but not her anger. She chided Walter, "You and your damned secret plots got a fine man killed. He didn't deserve this kind of death."

Walter took control of the charged environment, saying, "Perhaps you're correct. He was a secret agent and sudden death is one of the hazards of his profession." Not wanting to exacerbate the issue further, he snapped, "Sofia, we're in serious trouble. We've got to get out of here now. The maid will find the body and sound the alarm. The OVRA will know exactly what transpired; they will use all of their resources to capture us."

But Sofia did not hear him. Sofia was mentally and physically drained; she slumped onto her bed and stared blankly at Walter.

"Pull yourself together, Sofia. Take only the essentials."

Weakly, she replied, "Okay, Walter." But she remained in a daze, sitting on her bed unable to move or think coherently.

By now, other guests were awake and milling around in the hallway wondering where the sound of shots had come from.

"Sofia, get up!" With some vigor, he tapped her on the cheek. "Let's go. Now."

She became a little more robust. "Okay, Walter." She got up and slowly began to sort her possessions.

The hubbub in the hall alerted Walter that time was diminishing. He stepped into the hall and said to the small-assembled group, "Mister Segreti had an accident demonstrating how his Beretta 38 is such an excellent weapon. We are all okay." He forced a sardonic smile. "We'll have to fix that hole in the wall, however. It's all over now." He paused to regroup his thoughts. "Mister Segreti, embarrassed by the accident, made a quick exit from the *Signora's* suite. I suspect he is in the bar having a stiff drink."

A high-ranking Italian officer, a *generale di brigata*, approached Walter, and said, "Inexplicable events have been occurring in this hotel since your arrival, Mister Gregory. I want to see inside that suite."

"Very well, just as soon as *Signora* Russo recovers from the shock and is dressed properly to receive you, I'll let you know."

About this time, a scantily clad, gorgeous young woman went to the general, took his arm, and purred, "I'm cold. Come back to bed and rub my back."

The general looked at the woman and said, "It is no wonder." A slow smile crept across his weathered face. He took the woman's hand, patted her on her *derrière*, and said, "I'll see you later, Yank."

"Sure. Anytime." Walter released a deep sigh of relief that Joseph had done an excellent job of training his coterie of 'professional' women.

Walter wondered how many more narrow escapes they would have before they got out of the hotel. He went into Sofia's suite and saw she was fully recovered, dressed in her field clothes, and had her backpack by her side.

"I'm ready."

"But I'm not." Walter dashed into his room, strapped on his money belt, tossed one thousand lira on his bed, dressed in his field clothes, ensured the shards and the two canisters were in his backpack, and put his Smith and Wesson 38 revolver into his jacket pocket. He picked up his backpack, looked regretfully at his custom-made boots and his Stetson, snapped a military salute and muttered, "Goodbye, ol' pals. "

chapter thirteen

En route to the Red Sea, Abyssinia. 4 September 1937.

Walter and Sofia tossed their backpacks into the Auto Union Explorer. Sofia took the wheel and jammed her foot on the accelerator, propelling the Explorer out of the Goha Hotel's parking lot, and leaving a long string of skid marks. The tires caught purchase and the four-wheel-drive vehicle rapidly accelerated.

Walter urged, "Slow down, Sofia! We don't need to attract anyone's attention, especially the police."

"You're right. Thanks. My nerves are on edge." She slowed the vehicle to the posted speed limit. "How's that, pardner? After all, it's not every day that I kill an OVRA agent, sneak out of a hotel, and flee for my life."

Walter said calmly, "You drive, I'll navigate. Head west out of Axum to Adwa about thirty miles away."

"Very well." Sofia drove over the twisting road with deft skills on a moonless night. The headlights caught all manner of wildlife, including a couple of lionesses near the side of the road having a late dinner, with a young zebra for the main course.

"What route are we going to take to the Anglo-Egyptian Sudan? It's the safest area," Sofia asked.

"We're not going that way. We're going to Eritrea."

"Walter, are you nuts? That doesn't make sense. Eritrea is a province of Italian-controlled Abyssinia. I've had all of the OVRA I will ever need." She drove for a few minutes while Walter remained silent. "What's going on, Walter? Answer me or else I'm going to stop the Explorer and punch you in the nose. *Capisci?*"

Walter managed to suppress a small laugh. "I'm shaking in fear, my lady." He took advantage of her somewhat lightened mood. He wanted to reduce her anxiety while keeping the essential details secret, just in case the OVRA captured them. Finally, he related, "British and American intelligence have devised a plan for me *to* escape through Eritrea. And that's the way we're going. *Capiche?*"

"Walter Gregory, you're the most vexatious man I've ever met." She looked at him with a twisted smile. "You do infuriate me, but I'm going to trust you and your perfidious intelligence agencies who concocted this crazy scheme to get us out of here safely."

After they'd driven through Adwa, Walter said, "Pull over. I've got to get a specially prepared topographic map of this area out of my backpack."

"About time we figured out how we're going to get wherever we're going," Sofia teased. On reflection, she asked, "What is a 'specially prepared map'?"

"Questions, questions, questions," Walter chided Sofia. "This 'specially prepared map' is going to lead us to Allied territory. Trust me."

"Trust is all I've been doing these past few days. Now, I'm wanted for murder by a vicious secret police outfit, my career is in ruins, and I'm escaping with a nutcase Texan. How bad can it get?"

"Lots worse if the OVRA captures us." Walter retrieved the topographic map that Naval Intelligence had prepared for him. He snapped on his flashlight and studied the map for the secret route to his rendezvous on the Red Sea. After a few minutes, Walter had traced the route: They'd drive ahead on a twisting mountain road to Adigrat, turn north to Adi Caieh in Eritrea, and then northwest over what appeared to be an abandoned camel trail across the Rendakom Mountains to Arafali. It was a small fishing village located in a secluded cove of the Mits'iwa Channel on the Red Sea.

❧

Sofia's suite, Goha Hotel, Axum, Abyssinia. 5 September 1937.

Segreti knew he was dying. With steel resolve, he overcame the intense pain in his abdomen, and mustered his remaining strength to damn "that bitch" Sofia Savoy Russo. With the index finger on his right hand, he scribbled in his blood on the floor, "Russo" and "pgas can." An hour later, he expired.

By mid-morning, *Colonnello* Jacopo Visco was in Sofia's suite. He knelt on the floor, read Segreti's bloody message, inspected his body, rifled his pockets, and commented, "An oaf, but determined and absolutely loyal to our fascist cause."

He rose and said to his aide at the door, "It's clear now that *Signora* Russo and that American, Gregory, are spies." He wiped his hands on a face towel. "The mystery here is why the desk clerk Joseph was shot dead with Segreti's gun." His face twisted into a grimace of distaste. "Those two thugs have found at least one of our phosgene canisters and are escaping to one of the three British areas bordering us." It took only a second for Visco to conclude, "They're going to the Anglo-Egyptian Sudan to the west; and it's only about 300 miles if they travel on the main roads."

On an instant reflection, he spoke aloud, as if to his aide. "That route is too obvious. They'll leave a false trail toward the Sudan, and they'll head either southeast to the British Somaliland Protectorate or south to British East Africa. It's a much longer route, but the roads are better." He smiled with contempt. "I smell the deft hand of British intelligence in this escapade. The Americans are too stupid and timorous to pull off this sort of international intrigue." *Besides,* he reasoned, *Gregory was no fool and would not head for the Red Sea. He'd have to traverse Eritrea, a part of Italian East Africa. It's not feasible.*

At OVRA headquarters, *Colonnello* Visco issued orders for immediate action: "Two Anglo-type renegades have escaped Axum with valuable state property. They are driving a dark-green Auto Union Explorer automobile. Stop them at any cost and apprehend them. If that isn't possible, shoot to kill." He followed that with, "All border check points on extra vigilance. Patrol the back roads. Watch for tracks that lead into the bush."

Visco telephoned the commander of the *Regia Aeronautica Italia* aerodrome and asked him to send out airplanes to search for the two spies. The search areas he emphasized were the routes to the west and south.

About an hour later, the deafening roar of twelve Tri-Motor Savoia-Marchetti SM-79 bombers taking off filled the air with angry thunder. Their mission: Scout Abyssinia and find the escaping spies.

❧

In the dark night, with Sofia's skillful driving, the pair moved smartly and unfettered on the twisting main road to Adigrat. Walter was evaluating their odds of a successful escape. Towards dawn, he commented, "Sofia, even though we've got the head start and are headed in the direction the OVRA won't initially search, those advantages won't last long. *Colonnello* Visco is a smart cookie. By noon, he will have spread the alarm, and we will be hunted by the full force of the OVRA forces and Italian military, and many of the Abyssinians will want to report us for the huge reward I'm sure *Colonnello* Visco has posted."

❧

Early that morning, they were on a hard dirt trail that detoured around the town of Adigrat. Sofia was driving as they approached a creek bed with a steep bank that seemed to be dry. "What say you, Walter? Do we chance it?"

"Shut down. I'll inspect the bed to see how hard it is or find a more appropriate crossing." Walter walked atop the creek's steep bank for several hundred yards. He spotted a place where the bank was almost flat. He walked onto the creek bed trying to determine if it would support the weight of the Explorer.

Back at the Explorer he said, "There's a place down there where the bank is not sloped. My concern is, will that creek bed support the weight of the Explorer? If we don't try, we could be looking for a crossing all day. It's possible we'll never find an ideal crossing, and we don't have time to waste."

At the creek crossing, Walter engaged the four-wheel drive, put the regular drive shaft in a low gear, and eased the Explorer onto the creek bed. Walter's eyes narrowed and he clenched his teeth as the Explorer moved ever so slowly.

Sofia's hands were straining at the safety grips as she said silent prayers. Within a few feet of the far bank, Walter saw the bed ahead beginning to crack. The weight of the Explorer was projected forward. He pressed down on the accelerator ever so slightly to escape the crumbling crust, but to no avail. Within seconds, the rear wheels were bogged down in mud and the front wheels could not get enough purchase to pull the automobile forward. The Explorer was stuck.

Walter had significant experience driving well-serviced trucks in West Texas and knew what techniques had worked for him in similar situations. First, and perhaps most important, was not to spin the rear wheels. Such foolhardiness would sink the rear wheels even deeper, causing the differential to sink into the mud, and forcing the vehicle to high-center, making the extraction near impossible without a tow truck or other professional assistance.

With absolute assurance, he told Sofia, "Here's the situation. We've got to get as much brush as possible under those rear wheels to get the Explorer moving forward."

For the next thirty minutes, the pair used machetes to cut all the brush in the nearby area. They jammed it under the front and rear wheels as they laid out a path ahead toward the far bank. With perspiration dripping off them, Walter explained his plan. "I'm going to use the forward and reverse gears to rock the Explorer back and forth. When you see that I'm in the forward gear, push the vehicle forward with all your might. I'll continue the fast rocking, and with you pushing, we'll get out of here. *Capisci?*"

Apprehensive at their plight, she responded, "*Capisco*."

And so it began. At first, the forward and backward rocking of the Explorer, with Sofia pushing, did little to move the vehicle forward. Each time Walter changed the gears to forward, the rear wheels splattered sloppy mud onto Sofia. Nonetheless, she persevered and expended maximum effort to get the Explorer unstuck. Eventually, it moved almost imperceptibly forward. On the next forward thrust, the Explorer advanced about an inch. She let out a loud yelp.

Walter felt the forward movement, and was driven more intently to rock the Explorer faster and faster. The Explorer moved forward a couple of inches, then a foot, with mud flying. It then moved several feet. Sofia slipped into the black goop. Undaunted, she rose and pushed with all her reserve strength at the next forward movement. The front wheels got a firm purchase on the far bank and the Explorer shot forward out of the mud and onto the bank.

With the Explorer securely on hard ground, Walter leaped out of the Explorer and ran to the mud-covered Sofia. "Great work, *amico mio*."

He knelt beside her and kissed her mud-smeared face. "Yee haw, as we say in Texas." He smiled teasingly and said, "My, my young lady, aren't you the sophisticated fashion plate for this season?"

Almost too exhausted to respond, she smiled slyly and whispered, "I may have to castrate you, Walter Gregory. Here's another fine mess you've gotten me into."

chapter fourteen

A back road near Adigrat, Abyssinia. 6 September 1937.

As Walter and Sofia approached the town of Adigrat, they were driving on a rough and twisting dirt trail that ran several miles south of the main road. Walter said, "Let's stop—I'm parched and hungry. You?"

"Indeed," Sophia responded.

Walter drove the Explorer into a copse of myrrh trees. He climbed out, opened the rear door, and retrieved the water jug, a variety of dried fruit, and beef jerky. He set a table on the fold-down back door while whistling "Tea for Two."

Meanwhile, Sofia cracked the door handle and exited the vehicle. "I need to get out and stretch." She stomped her boots on the ground to stimulate the blood in her feet. "The pounding we've had in this iron monster has severely assaulted my *derrière*," she said through pursed lips. Then she began to massage her backside vigorously. She relaxed and looked coyly at Walter, "Please excuse me as I rub my rear end to iron out the bumps."

Walter cracked a wicked smile, rubbed his hands together salaciously, and quipped, "May I help, *signora*?"

"Indeed not, you masher." Sofia twirled in a complete circle, and with a seductive twinkle in her eyes, she purred, "Perhaps another day, *signore*." A few minutes later, she drained her canteen, and then ate a couple strips of jerky and a handful of the dried fruit.

Refreshed, she said, "That fare was not champagne and caviar, but it was delicious."

"Enough?"

"I'm much better—almost human. Let's get going."

Before Walter started the vehicle, he perused his map and said with apprehension, "We'll have to hit the main highway and go through Adigrat. It's about four miles ahead after we're on that road."

"Why? What's on that map for you to make such a dangerous decision, pardner?"

"Two things, pardner: We need petrol, and just on the east side of town is the Baraka River. It's wide, deep, and roaring. The only way we'll get across is to use the bridge on the main road." He double-checked the map and saw that a mile or so beyond the river, the road made a left turn and ran north to Adi Caieh. He retrieved his magnifying glass and studied the topographic map intently. "There are no other options. We will have to stay on the main road until we reach the Eritrean border—about ten miles north of here. Not the best scheme, but it's our only option." He stored his tools and the map. "You game?"

Sofia seemed pensive. "We're going to expose our hand. But if we must, we must." She checked her watch. "It's mid-afternoon. Any estimate when the OVRA will know our route and where we've been?"

"By now, there must be a nationwide manhunt for us." Walter looked at Sofia with intense and sympathetic eyes. "To answer your question directly, I reckon that *Colonnello* Visco will know shortly after we leave Adigrat. Then he'll direct all his forces on our tail."

With the realization that they might well be on a fool's errand, and that their freedom was in serious peril, Sofia said, "Walter, we've no time to dilly-dally. Let's get our rears in gear and get moving. Time is a' wasting, as they say in Texas. *Vero?*"

"Then I reckon we oughta skedaddle from here." Walter engaged the gears and moved out to the main road. "My lady, here goes nothing. Keep your fingers crossed."

"I'll send a prayer to Saint Joseph and ask for his protection."

ℰℑ

About thirty minutes later, the Auto Union Explorer, with a full tank of petrol, was cruising north at reduced speed on the twisting mountain road. Walter commented, "That was painless, and no *carabinieri* are on our tail. Nonetheless, I'll wager that the telephone is ringing in *Colonnello* Visco's office."

The next thirty minutes are crucial, he thought. *When we get across the Eritrean border—a Muslim province—our odds of a success-ful escape will improve a little.* Walter did not want to worry Sofia so he said only, "After we enter Eritrea, we'll hit the backcountry again for most of the way over some rough mountain terrain to Adi Caieh. Keep your fingers crossed that my special map is accurate."

As they rounded a sharp curve on the narrow, two-lane, moun-tain road, Walter shouted, "Police roadblock ahead. There's no way around it. Those two *carabinieri* have spotted us." He stopped the Explorer about one hundred fifty feet from the roadblock. "Sofia, do exactly what I tell you to do. No smart cracks. No questions."

"Yes, Walter," Sofia responded, as fear raced through her body. "What are we going to do, Walter? Is this the end of our adventure and us?"

"No!" he almost shouted. In a hoarse whisper, "We have one option, and only one option. We are going to kill those two *carabin-ieri*. It's either them or us."

She stared at him with dubious eyes. "I can't do it," Sofia exclaimed. "It's cold-blooded murder." She looked through the windshield and saw the *carabinieri* approaching the Explorer at a measured pace. Their eyes were focused intently on Walter and Sofia, one man on each side of their vehicle. The *carabinieri* held their Beretta MAB-38 submachine guns at the ready.

"Sofia, get ready with your Beretta 32. They know who we are." Walter drew his Smith and Wesson 38 and tucked it by his right hip.

"Stop it, Walter! I can't do it." Perplexed by the impending deadly confrontation, Sofia was racked with fear and indecision, her conflicting strict moral code and conflicting survival instincts. Terror and doubt clouded her mind. "They are my countrymen, and they have done me no wrong." She closed her eyes, as if the impending crisis didn't exist.

"Sofia!" Walter shouted. "Either kill that fellow approaching your side of this vehicle or spend the remaining few weeks of your life in an OVRA prison, and die a lingering and painful death."

She looked at Walter with terror-glazed eyes. "What am I to do, Walter? Give me strength."

"Your Beretta is your strength." Walter cocked the hammer on his 38.

The click, click of this motion sent an immediate message to Sofia. She drew her Beretta 32, snapped back the receiver, and let it slam forward to chamber a round.

The *carabinieri* were at the front fenders, with their index fingers on the triggers of their submachine guns.

Walter instructed, "Hold your Beretta in your left hand and below the window sill. When that fellow motions for you to roll down your window, do it quickly, and smile at him. He'll stick his head inside to question you and ask for your papers. Without thought, blaze away and empty your magazine into his face."

Sofia stared at the *carabiniere* standing next to her door as he made motions for her to roll down her window. She froze with inaction, staring at the fellow with blank eyes.

Walter's 38 spoke with a tremendous blast that reverberated throughout the Explorer. The *carabiniere* on his side fell away with a neat round hole between his dead eyes. Walter cracked open his door to exit and to pick up the *carabiniere's* weapon and magazine clips.

The *carabiniere* on Sofia's side slammed the butt of his weapon into the window, smashing it to smithereens. He jammed his submachine gun inside, with the barrel pointed at Walter. His finger tightened on the trigger. Sofia cried, "You won't kill Walter!" Without thinking and with the quickness of a rattlesnake strike, she thrust her Beretta under the fellow's chin and fired, and fired, and fired. Blood splattered on her jacket and the man without a face fell away. She screamed and screamed, dropped her gun, buried her face in her hands, and sobbed hysterically.

Walter moved to take her in his arms, but Sofia had coiled into a fetal position. He uncurled her, wrapped his arms around her, and let her sob. After a time, her sobbing eased somewhat. At a loss as to how to comfort her, he said sympathetically, "Well done, Sofia."

Sofia pulled away from Walter, glared at him, and snapped, "I hate you, Walter Gregory! You idiot Texan." Through her sobs she muttered, "Now I'm guilty of another murder, and that fellow's blood is splattered all over my jacket."

"You saved our lives. That took courage," he said.

Several minutes later, she wiped her tears and stared at Walter with intense eyes. "Thanks, Walter, my paladin, my pardner. It's you that saved my life once again."

"We'll need that fellow's weapon and ammunition." He moved around the front of the Explorer to Sofia's side and retrieved the dead man's submachine gun and clips. He said, as he entered the vehicle, "I reckon that this is just the beginning of our gunplay. Let me show you how to operate this weapon."

಄

After Walter's instructions, Sofia felt skilled and confident as she cradled the Beretta MAB-38 submachine guns in her lap. "I'm ready. Be assured, I won't freeze next time."

"I know."

A few miles farther on, Walter pulled off the highway, engaged the four-wheel gears, and found the narrow camel trail noted on his special map. It was about four miles east of the highway. Walter could only average only about eight miles per hour over the rough trail.

"What now, mighty warrior?"

Walter was flummoxed. He had no response. He consulted his special map and said, "With luck, we'll reach the outskirts of Adi Caieh before sundown."

"You don't fool me, Walter Gregory. What's going on in that stubborn head of yours?"

"When *Colonnello* Visco gets the report on those two dead *carabinieri,* he'll know exactly where we are, that we're traveling on a back road in the bush, and that we're headed for a Red Sea port. Without doubt, he'll issue a 'Kill on sight' command and personally lead the hunt for us."

About ten miles later, they were carefully inching along the deeply rutted road. Sofia spotted a pride of lions ahead, blocking the road: five lionesses, several cubs, and a massive, angry male. Walter stopped the Explorer about a hundred feet in front of the pride. "What now?"

Sofia leaned toward the windshield and said, "Those cubs are so cute."

"So be it, but that brute of a male does not cotton to our intrusion. He's going to challenge this noisy metal monster of ours. That's his pride and he's going to defend it to the death."

The lion's eyes focused on the Explorer as he advanced slowly and roared threateningly. Soon he was within a few feet of the Explorer. He roared and roared, telling the metal monster, *This is my pride and my trail. Get out of here or I will rip you apart.*

Walter realized that they were in a classic 'Mexican standoff.' In a minute, Walter faltered. "Okay big boy, you win." He turned the Explorer left, off the trail, to circle around this brave fellow and his harem. Slowly, he made a wide go-around, leaving the pride intact. The male followed the Explorer until it was evident that it was no longer a threat.

Several hours later, the sun was very low on the horizon and the shadows were long. The trail had smoothed to the point that Walter had the Explorer in two-wheel drive and was averaging about twenty miles per hour. To their left, the flickering lights of Adi Caieh reflected off the low-lying cumulus clouds.

Sofia's head nodded in a light sleep.

"Sofia, it's getting late and we ought to shut down for the night," Walter said. He drove the Explorer deep into a cluster of trees.

"All right, coach. Call the *maître d'hôtel* to set our table, and the *ménage* to turn down the bed in our penthouse suite."

Satiated and exhausted, the pair slept arm in arm in the back of the Explorer.

chapter fifteen

A back road, west of Adi Caieh, Abyssinia. 7 September 1937.

Surprisingly, the camel trail was relatively smooth as Walter headed east toward the Rendakom Mountains, about fifteen miles ahead. His special map indicated a small mountain trail as passage to the Red Sea and Arafali, the small fishing village in a secluded cove on the Mits'iwa Channel. They were to meet Aamir Sanawbar; he was ostensibly a fisherman, but was actually a smuggler, and in the employ of the British intelligence service MI6. Sanawbar carried narcotics, alcohol, and other contraband from Eritrea across the Red Sea to the British Crown Colony of Aden, and brought munitions and British agents into Eritrea. Beneath the fish storage area was a small compartment where he stashed his contraband.

The Explorer kicked up a cloud of dust as it moved over the trail at ten miles per hour. Walter's and Sofia's morale soared as the mountains came ever closer. Once in the mountains, on this back trail unknown to OVRA, their odds of escape would escalate significantly.

ℭ

OVRA Headquarters, Axum, Abyssinia. 7 September 1937.

Colonnello Visco leaned back in his chair, lit a cigarette, and stared at the ceiling. The nagging notion in the back of his mind ached to blast to the fore. The nicotine nettled his thoughts. He mused. *Something is amiss. This scenario has a twist that escapes me. What am I missing?* He inhaled deeply and slowly let the smoke drift upward. *It makes no sense: The Americans overfly this country with their photographic reconnaissance aeroplanes; they send that spy Gregory here. Signora Russo and Gregory are in cahoots. My cryptographers reported intercepts of unusual and deeply coded transmissions emanating from the British in Aden, Port Said, Sallah, and London—their code not broken. It is clear that not all this activity occurred to find phosgene canisters in a vague location that they were uncertain even existed. No. Something much more important is afoot.* His mind whirled as if he were viewing a passing newsreel movie of possible scenarios. Nothing fit. Exasperated, he mumbled, "It's that dammed MI6. Nothing is straightforward with those *testa di cazzi*, always putting false clues, dead ends, and other deceptions in their operations!"

Colonnello Visco leaned forward on his desk and pounded it hard with his left fist several times in uncontrolled anger. He snapped to his aide, "They killed two of my men in cold blood." With unbridled hate in his eyes, he picked up the secret message that informed him of the murders, their location, and the heading of Walter's Explorer. He walked to a large map of Abyssinia on the far wall, and studied intently the area where Walter and Sofia had last been seen. After a minute he quipped, "Clearly, they are headed for a Red Sea port where British intelligence will, no doubt, evacuate them with our phosgene canister." He picked up a ten-power magnifying glass and studied the topography of the Rendakom Mountains. "How are they going to cross the Rendakom Mountains? They are not stupid enough to try to cross on the main highway out of Asmera, which is far to the north. We will have that pass blocked. They must have a secret route through this mountain range, supplied by British intelligence."

He continued studying the mountain range but could not see any passage through it. "This map is worthless. Look at the map's legend: Data accurate as of 1906. Royal Geographical Society. Scale is 1:250,000."

With a sudden revelation he spouted, "Now I understand that diplomatic folderol several months ago when those United States Navy planes flew over that area. They were taking aerial photographs. I am certain American intelligence prepared a special map for Walter Gregory. Photographic interpreters found a route through this mountain range for his escape to the Red Sea. But which port?" *I should have pieced this puzzle together much sooner.*

Colonnello Visco telephoned the commanding officer of the aerodrome. "Gregory and Russo are headed for the Rendakom Mountains on a back trail—somewhere east of Adi Caieh. Get as many airplanes in the air as you can to spot that Explorer and destroy it. Have a Caproni Ca-310 ready to take me to Adi Caieh. I want the fastest twin-engine airplane you have, yes? I'll set up a command post at our offices in the city. Relay all reports to me there as FLASH priority messages."

He listened as the commanding officer acknowledged his requests. "Very well. I'll be at your operations office in about twenty minutes. Have that Ca-310 ready for immediate takeoff."

He turned to his aide *Maggiore* Belli, and instructed, "Have all OVRA resources in the area assemble at my command post in Adi Caieh, and alert the second squad of the Black Flag Company to set up a road block at the entrance to the mountain pass on the highway east of Decamere."

"*Si, Colonnello. Immediatmente.*"

இ

The cloud of dust behind the Explorer reached high into the sky in the still air as Walter drove at a steady pace toward the mountain range. "Those mountains are only about four miles away. We're gonna make it, pardner."

Sofia grabbed Walter's arm and flashed her largest smile. "Thank God. And you, Walter." They continued in silence as the miles slipped by.

The *rat-tat-tat-tat, rat-tat-tat-tat* staccato of machine gun bullets ripping into the running board on the driver's side and front fender of their Explorer jolted the pair into the reality that the *Regia Aeronautica Italia* had found them, and that they probably were not going to make it. At very low altitude, an Italian tri-motor bomber, the Savoia-Marchetti SM-79, zoomed past.

Walter hit the brakes and shouted, "Get out! Get your backpack and submachine gun, and run for that copse of myrrh trees on the right. Now!"

Sofia needed no additional motivation. In a flash, she moved to the copse.

The SM-79 was in a wide turn to make another strafing run.

Walter grabbed his equipment and ran with all his strength to catch up with Sofia. He clutched her arm and together they plunged deep into the copse. Breathing hard, the pair collapsed to the ground and grabbed each other for support.

A thousand yards in front of the Explorer, the SM-79 was lined up for another strafing pass and it began its run at an altitude of no more than five hundred feet. The roar of the three motors on the SM-79 filled the air. Twin machine guns opened fire and bullets ripped into the Explorer, blowing the tires, chewing up the hot radiator, blasting out the windows, and ripping the hood off; then tracers hit the Explorer's petrol tank and the vehicle exploded in a mass of flames and flying metal.

With absolute resignation, Walter said, "There goes our transportation and most of our gear and supplies." He scanned the flaming scene with binoculars and saw with unfettered detail the devastation to the Explorer and surrounding area. "Reckon we can hail a taxicab?"

A dour Sofia responded, "You are not funny, Texan."

The tri-motor SM-79 made several more low passes over the remains of the Explorer to confirm the kill and try to spot any corpses.

Walter sat up, returned the binoculars to his backpack, and commented, "We can be assured that the radio operator in that SM-79 is now broadcasting their position and a damage assessment report to OVRA headquarters. *Colonnello* Visco will have that message in a few minutes, and he'll dispatch an OVRA special squad to recover our bodies or else get on our trail. I estimate that they'll be here in four or five hours."

"All right, Sofia, Act One is over and OVRA wins the point." He lifted Sofia off the ground and hugged her tightly. "We're gonna make it. Texans are ornery bastards and always win the second and final act."

Tears sprang into her eyes. "How, Walter?" Her voice choked to almost a whisper. Suppressing her angst, she squeezed him tightly and kissed him on his cheeks and mouth. With her resolve almost restored, she cracked, "So what's your plan, big boy?" As she released him, she picked up her backpack and submachine gun. "I reckon we gotta hike to them there hills," she said, mocking his Texas bravado. "Let's skedaddle."

"You got it, pardner," Walter responded with a forced smile. He looked at his map and said, "We'll be in the open for about two hours, with absolutely no cover. However, once we hit the base of those mountains, we'll have some protection. Our most important advantage is that the *Colonnello* Visco doesn't know where we'll enter or exit those mountains." He picked up his gear and looked at Sofia with intense eyes, knowing the danger in the wide-open plain that awaited them. "Let's get our rumps in gear and start walking."

"Very well, *Commandante*."

Walter picked up his gear and shouldered his submachine gun. "When the OVRA scouts don't find our remains, *Colonnello* Visco will have a reasonably accurate assessment of where we are and where we're headed. He'll send mobile patrols and pursuit aircraft after us."

Hand in hand they left their hiding spot and hiked toward the mountains looming high in the distance. The pair hiked with a steady, powerful pace. The ground began to slant upward, gently at first, then slightly more steeply. Walter spotted a small trail that lead to the base of the mountains and then vanished into the gray, granite rocks.

⚓

Meanwhile, aviators from the 81ᵃ *Squadriglia* filed into the briefing room singly and in pairs. Soon, they filled the room, awaiting their target assignments and other details of the upcoming mission. *Tenente* Fione Lazzari sat upright in his seat near the back and anxiously wondered what Muslim rebel target the intelligence office would assign to him for his first combat mission.

In short order, the squadron commander entered and the intelligence officer called, "*Attenzione.*" The room vibrated with the din of scraping chairs, shuffling boots, and the rattle of aviation equipment as the aircrew men snapped to attention.

The commander scanned the combat veterans and the untried novices; he felt assured that the men of his squadron would accomplish their critical mission. He recalled the *Segretissimo* (Top Secret) FLASH message from *Generale* Rodolfo Graziani, Marshal of Italian East Africa, and his imperative orders to stop the escaping spies at any cost.

The commander ordered, "Stand down." Again, the room vibrated with the cacophonous rumble of the aircrews adjusting their gear, and sitting. The commander continued, "*Generale* Graziani has ordered our squadron on a critical mission—one that is vital to the Kingdom of Italy and our *Fascismo* government. Failure is not acceptable, no matter the reason. Now, listen carefully to the intelligence officer as he briefs us for the mission."

The intelligence officer unveiled a large map that covered the area from Axum to the Red Sea and from the Anglo-Egyptian Sudan to British East Africa. "Gentlemen, today your mission is search and destroy."

Tenente Lazzari's heart raced with keen anticipation. *At last, an opportunity to prove my mettle.*

"Your mission is to find two spies and gun them down. You'll patrol in two-airplane sections, a veteran pilot and a novice in each section. Our latest intelligence confirms that the spies are traveling on foot and are somewhere between Adi Caieh and the Rendakom Mountains." He used his pointer to indicate the spies' approximate position. He paused to scan his briefing cards. "These spies are resourceful and are armed with two handguns and perhaps two submachine guns. They must be stopped before they reach a British-controlled area and reveal some of our country's top secret intelligence. Show no mercy."

Tenente Lazzari's eagerness began to fade: *No real action against the rebels today.*

The briefer dropped a clear plastic sheet outlining the patrol areas over the map. "We don't know in which direction they are headed. The Anglo-Egyptian Sudan is their most likely choice, British East Africa is our second estimate. We doubt that they'll attempt to trust the French in Afars and Issas, and access to British Somaliland is too difficult." In synchronization with his words, he used the pointer to indicate the locales he named. "Perhaps they'll try to traverse the Rendakom Mountains, but that's unlikely because the OVRA controls all roads across, and it would be near impossible to transverse these mountains on foot. OVRA patrols are roving the countryside in support of our efforts."

Capitano Orlando Costa, a veteran of the Cyrenaica and Abyssinian campaigns, asked, "What have these spies done to cause such a hubbub, who are they?"

"Captain Costa, I've said all that matters about their transgressions. Suffice it to say they have betrayed our *Fascismo* cause. We must find them, kill them, and recover our secrets—failure is not an option."

Capitano Costa continued, "We understand that. But who are they? If we are going to assassinate them, we ought to know who our victims are." He arose for emphasis. "Surely you can tell us. *No?*"

Resigned, the intelligence officer responded, "Very well. The man is Walter Gregory, an American secret agent. The female is an Italian citizen and a professor at the University of Rome."

With this tease of information, Lazzari sat forward in his chair with all his senses attuned.

"The woman is from one of Italy's most respected families and is the second cousin of King Victor Savoy Emmanuel III. Sofia Savoy Russo is a traitor to her country."

Tenente Lazzari gasped loudly, threw his hands to his face, and tried to suppress a doleful wail as he slumped deeply in his chair.

His fellow aviators stared at him with questioning eyes. The intelligence officer ordered, "*Tenente* Lazzari, be quiet and pay attention. What's the matter with you? If you have a question, speak as a professional."

Lazzari recovered enough to rise, stand at attention, and articulate, "My apologies, sir. *Mi scusi.*"

The intelligence officer continued his briefing with the weather report; survival, evasion, resistance and escape (SERE) tactics, should anyone be downed near rebel-controlled areas; survival and rescue options (SAR); call signs, radio frequencies, and a host of other detailed information.

At the conclusion of the briefing and after the question-and-answer period, the commanding officer rose, made the two-airplane assignments, and assigned each pair their search sector. About midway through, he spotted Lazzari. "*Tenente* Lazzari, you will be *Capitano* Costa's wing man."

Lazzari rose, as fear and confusion racked his soul. He responded in a faint voice, "*Si, capisco, il mio commandante.*"

"I'm counting on you, *Tenente* Lazzari, to do your duty faithfully on this, your first combat mission. *Capitano* Costa will be your mentor. Do as he says and you'll do fine."

In the meantime, the plane captains had completed their final checks of the Fiat CR32, open-cockpit biplanes scheduled for the day's mission. Included were a myriad of other details to ensure the airplanes were in first-class condition: fuel and oil tanks full, radios functional, machine guns armed, ammunition belts stored properly, engines started, and oil pressure up.

Soon, *Tenente* Fione Lazzari approached his Fiat, as its propeller ticked over slowly. He completed his walk-around and found all external systems operational. He climbed into the cockpit, buckled his safety belt, and completed his preflight check. On the hand signal from *Capitano* Costa, he inched the throttle forward, the engine roared, and the two Fiat pursuit airplanes lifted off in tight formation.

✧

"Time," Walter said. "Only sip a few swallows, we need to conserve our water supply. Let's relax while I try to decipher the passage through these mountains from our special map."

"You do that, big-boy Texan. I'm gonna sit on my *derrière*, drink as you so masterfully directed, snack on that chef-prepared beef jerky, and wait patiently right here as you try to figure out how to save me." She grinned with false bravado at Walter and pulled out her canteen.

The faint hum of two Fiat pursuit planes in the distance finally registered with Walter. He leaped up and shouted, "Sofia, get up and scatter."

"What?" She looked up at Walter. "What's happening?"

"There are two pursuit planes coming, obviously looking for us." He slung his submachine gun off his shoulder and charged a round. "Damn! We'll be spotted on this wide-open plain. Hear them?"

"Yes. Now I do."

"Scatter! And hit the deck. Together we make a large target. Singly, we'll be harder to spot."

The pair ran in opposite directions, and when they were about fifty yards apart, they fell to the ground face up. Sofia charged her submachine gun.

The two Fiat pursuit planes were at two thousand feet and headed east toward the Rendakom Mountains. *Tenente* Lazzari had positioned his Fiat slightly behind, to the right, and above *Capitano* Costa's plane. Costa spoke into his throat microphone, "Lazzari, see that burned-out hulk of the spies' automobile?"

"*Si. Io vedo.*"

"I'm going to search to the north. You stay on course and scout the mountain range and the area to the south." He banked his Fiat to the left, and commanded, "Go to five hundred feet in that open plain."

"*Si, signore.*"

Lazzari eased back the throttle and his Fiat slowly descended. At five hundred feet, he started an expanded-square search pattern. In just a few moments, he spotted the two spies lying in the grass. He slowed his Fiat to ninety miles per hour—just a notch above stall speed, charged his two Breda 7.7mm machine guns, and banked sharply over Walter. In the next instant, the stark realization that he was about to kill Sofia and her escort overwhelmed his essence. *It's Sofia and the American.*

He straightened his Fiat, gained some altitude, and flew to the mountains. Confusion reigned in his soul. He was torn between his duty to his country as a soldier, and his responsibility as a human. His angst and frustration were maddening. In an impetuous attempt to ease his pain, he sighted an outcropping in the mountains, drove his Fiat toward it, and fired a long burst from both machine guns. The rock formation exploded into thousands of pieces.

Lazzari sharply banked his Fiat and returned to the plain at five hundred feet. Walter saw the Fiat flying low and slow toward him, and reckoned that the pilot would begin firing at any time. Walter hoisted his submachine gun, led the Fiat, and fired a long burst. A few rounds ripped into the Fiat's empennage and some fabric, and an interior strut flew off. *Damn, that does it. I didn't lead my aim enough. He's okay. Get him, Sofia.*

The Fiat's damage was slight, and Lazzari flew to where Sofia lay. He inched the throttle back a bit to lose altitude and banked the Fiat into a ninety-degree turn over her. Hoping that she would realize that he was not going to shoot, he waved his left arm vigorously.

Sofia had gotten her clue when she saw Walter fire. She did not know what this crazy pilot was doing and thought he might be teasing them before his *coup de gràce*. She aimed her submachine gun slightly ahead of the Fiat and fired a full clip. Several of her rounds punctured the petrol tank in the upper wing, and the volatile liquid spilled onto the hot engine. The petrol instantly erupted into searing flames and the prop wash thrust the conflagration to the cockpit, consuming the aviator and the Fiat. In a second or so, the Fiat spun crazily, slammed into the ground and exploded in flames and flying pieces.

Walter shouted, "Nice shooting, *mi amigo*. You saved our lives." He rose and trotted to her.

"Not so nice, Walter. I've just killed another human and my countryman. I'm a cold-blooded killer. What have I become?"

Walter sat next to Sofia, hugged her tightly, and spoke, "You are a heroine. You've saved our lives—again. You've eliminated another fascist—for the good of humanity."

"I don't feel like a heroine. I'm not." She made the sign of the cross. "I pray for that man's soul." After a short time, she rose with effort, "Let's get out of here. I need to walk."

"Let's go. More *Regia Aeronautic Italiana* aircraft will be in this area soon."

They soon reached the narrow ravine that would lead them into the mountains. Walter consulted his map. "Clearly, the aerial photographs from which this map was made could not resolve the deterioration of the trail into this narrow ravine's footpath. Maybe it's an old camel trail, or perhaps a goat trail. There's no way any vehicle could traverse this mountain range from this point onward."

He showed the map to Sofia. "From what I can tell, we head up this ravine on this goat trail until we're deep into the mountains. There I see a trail that seems to be more distinct. It follows gaps and streams through the mountains. After we pass the summit, the downhill trail is wider and we ought to see the Red Sea." He folded the map and jammed it into his coat pocket. "We ought to get as far up this trail as we can before nightfall. Ready to move, *Signora* Doctor Sofia Savoy Russo?"

"*Si, paisano* Walter Gregory." She stood and began to hike up the trail. "Let's move, Texan. Time's a' wastin.'"

chapter sixteen

The Rendakom Mountains, Eritrea. 7 September 1937.

for several hours, Walter and Sofia hiked the narrow, steep, and twisting trail. Soon, long shadows fell into the ravine and the trail became engulfed in deep shade. They hiked cautiously along the indistinct trail. Before long, near blackness covered their footing.

Walter, in the lead, realized that it was too dangerous to continue in the fast-fading light. Exhausted, he raised his hand in the universal signal to stop. He turned and asked, "Sofia, how ya doin'?"

"I'm done." She plopped down on a small outcropping and leaned back against the mountain's hard granite. "Water, please, *amico mio*." She drew her canteen and almost drained it. She sighed and commented, "Best wine I've ever tasted."

Walter sat beside her, patted her knee, and remarked between sharp, measured breaths, "You are doing great. Best mountaineer I've ever hiked with."

Sofia looked at him with one eye closed and the other raised in mocking disbelief. She snapped, "You are a liar, Walter Gregory. You damn well know that I'm a drag on your progress through this malevolent mountain range. Will it never end?" She leaned against him and began to rub his back.

After a few minutes, Walter felt slightly refreshed from some swigs of water. He rose and told Sofia, "I'm going up the trail a bit to see if there is a wide place where we can stretch out and sleep."

He went around a couple of sharp bends and found a wide cutout in the side of the mountain. It was not an ideal place to spend the night, but it was handy and far better than the narrow trail. He went to Sofia, told her of his find, and carefully escorted her to the place. They drank their remaining water in silence, and ate dried fruit and beef jerky.

After their sparse meal, they snuggled together arm in arm for reassurance and warmth. Both were gravely aware that the OVRA was probably on their trail. Nonetheless, sleep came quickly on the hard rock bed.

☙

Earlier, *Colonnello* Visco, in his command post in Adi Caieh, had read the radio message from the Savoia-Marchetti SM-79. He saw that the crew had destroyed the Explorer, but had not seen any bodies. However, the rear gunner, *Sergenta* Egidio Santelli, reported that he had caught a glimpse of two people running into a copse of trees on his right.

Colonnello Visco commented to *Capitano* Dante Caito, with an odious eagerness in his voice, "I will lead your detail of alpine troops personally. Apparently, the two spies escaped the strafing." He was pleased in a perverse way. "Since they are trapped between the Rendakom Mountains and me, I want them alive for interrogation."

He checked his map carefully. "They will walk on that old trail to the mountains. See here, *Capitano*." His index finger traced a path from the copse of trees to the base of the mountains. "There appears to be a small ravine at the base of that trail and Allied intelligence must have discovered a passage through the mountains starting there. What I don't know is, where the trail exits on the coast. Accordingly, we must overtake them in the mountains. *Capisci?*" Visco folded his map and placed it in his valise. "They have a six- or seven-hour head start. Let's move out."

"I have four transport trucks loaded with my men and one radio command truck ready."

"Excellent, *Capitano.*"

෴

At first light, Walter and Sofia, after a short repast, began their upward hike. At a sharp bend in the trail, Walter looked back and saw the plain and the copse of trees they had left the day before. Walter saw some sort of movement, and retrieved his binoculars. At the base of the ravine, he spotted the five OVRA trucks. He scanned the trail, and saw twenty-four soldiers hiking up the trail, led by a senior officer. He realized they were gaining on them fast and assumed they were special alpine troops.

"Sofia, we've got company coming up the trail—only about three hours behind us." Not having met *Colonnello* Visco, he passed the binoculars to Sofia. "Recognize that officer leading those alpine troops?" Walter pointed to a spot near a massive outcropping overhanging the trail.

She took the binoculars, focused the diopter ring to match her eyes' focus, and scanned the trail. "It is *Colonnello* Visco in the flesh. That *bastardo!* He is driven to get us one way or another."

There was no need for either of them to comment further. They picked up their gear and shoved off at a quick pace. Three hours later, the pair was lagging; thirst gripped their throats; their leg muscles ached; and their morale was sinking.

Walter urged Sofia to push harder. "Come on, *paisano.* We've got to increase the distance between us and those OVRA troops."

"Walter, stop!" Sofia pleaded. "I can't go any farther." She dropped to the hard, granite trail and stretched out in a spread eagle. She took deep breaths of the fresh mountain air and closed her eyes.

Walter sat beside her and rubbed her calf muscles. "All right, we'll take a ten-minute break." Neither spoke; conserving their energy was paramount.

Walter timed their break with his watch. At exactly the ten-minute mark he rose, scanned the lower trail with his binoculars, and saw that the OVRA alpine troops were much closer—only about ninety minutes behind, he guessed. "Sofia, get up! We've got to get the lead out of our butts and get moving. Those troops are well trained and conditioned for an alpine environment."

Walter helped Sofia rise. "*Paisano,* put one foot in front of the other. Then repeat. And repeat again. We've got to move faster."

"I'll try, but I'm seriously fatigued and dehydrated. My muscles are incredibly stiff." She made maximum effort to maintain pace with Walter's fast clip. After a few minutes, she grabbed Walter and looked at him with wide, startled eyes. "If it comes to the showdown, Walter, you must leave me and save yourself with those canisters and radio-active shards. I'll take a host of those *bastardos* with my machine gun before they get me."

"Nonsense, Sofia. Utter nonsense. We will either escape together or die together. *Capisci, paisano?* Deal?"

With soft tears in her eyes, Sofia murmured, "No deal, Walter Gregory. Your mission is far more important than my small life." She wiped her eyes. "You know what I said is absolutely true. I don't want any of your male bravado causing the Allies to lose this coming war." She paused for effect. "You do as I say, or else I will kill you."

Walter was somewhat dumfounded that his moral code was challenged wholeheartedly with clear, feminine logic. He nodded his head and looked away. "Enough of this talk. Both of us will make it. Texans and their *compañeras* are resourceful, skillful, and deceitful to a fare-thee-well."

"Walter, my *caro amicomio,* if all else fails, promise me on your mother's grave that you'll save your last bullet for me. I refuse to let *Colonnello* Visco capture me. I will not be raped and tortured to death in his OVRA prison." She put her hands on his cheeks and kissed him full on the mouth. "Promise me, Walter. Promise me."

Walter blinked at the stark realization at what could very well be his last honorable duty. He squeezed Sofia against his body and nodded slowly in the affirmative.

Sofia broke from his embrace and snapped, "Walter Gregory, I hate you. Now kiss me with all the passion you've got in you. *Comprendere?*"

Very slowly, she matched his breathing.

⁊

The pair struggled to make headway on the steep and frequently narrow trail that caused them to hike single file. Walter rigged a rope to tie them together.

It was soon obvious that the OVRA's alpine troops were gaining rapidly and the confrontation was only about a half-hour away. On the now very narrow trail, where every step portended a fatal fall, the pair rounded a steep turn, and Sofia spotted a small ravine to her right. It was partially hidden by a giant, overhead outcropping and thick bushes. It intersected their trail at about a thirty-degree angle, making a sharp V-shaped junction.

"Walter! Look. Perhaps we can hide in that ravine and ambush those fascists."

"We'll get a few, but in the end, we will either be dead or wounded and captured. No deal."

Walter carefully pushed away the bushes and saw that a small stream flowed in the ravine, which ran toward the plain, its base south of the OVRA trucks, perhaps by a couple of miles. He hiked about a hundred yards down the ravine, and realized that they might be able to trek down it and enter the plain. "Sofia, we've got a chance—a life-saving stratagem."

"What chance, Walter? Those alpine troops are getting closer."

Walter explained, "I'm going to execute an old Comanche Indian gambit. We are going to get behind our pursuers and escape after they follow the false trail I will leave ahead on our original trail. Enter that ravine and try not to disturb the entrance too much. Stay there and be prepared. I'm going ahead for about a thousand feet to leave clues that will indicate that we are still ahead of them."

In a few seconds, he was out of Sofia's sight. He purposely tumbled rocks to expose those less weather-beaten; he snapped twigs on bushes, and brushed against a sharp outcropping to tear off a small piece of his trousers and leave fresh blood.

Within a few minutes, he was at Sofia's side. "Let's fill our canteens and move out."

"I'm way ahead of you, buster." Sofia stood, got her gear, and started downhill on this new trail. The hiking was relatively easy. "You are reasonably clever for an *Americano*, I must say. What then?"

"We are gonna be bandits, real blackguards. We are going to swipe one of their trucks and high tail it out of here."

"And drive over this mountain range in a Zeppelin or perhaps with magic powers, I assume?"

"No. We are going to Asmera and across these mountains on the main road."

"You're nuts, Walter Gregory. But I reckon that I'm tied to you and with no other options at hand. Lead on."

About four hours later, the pair was at the base of the mountain range and about two miles south of their original starting point. Walter used his binoculars and spotted the five multi-wheeled trucks parked at the base of the first ravine.

"The question is, did they leave guards at those trucks? We'll have to assume so."

Carefully, the pair advanced toward the trucks. Frequently, Walter checked the area for guards or motion of any kind. He did not see any. Feeling more confident, the pair moved faster, with their submachine guns at the ready. In a few minutes, they were lying in thick grass one hundred feet from the trucks. "Sofia, one of those trucks is a command truck. I see radio antennae on its roof. But I just don't see any guards. It's almost inconceivable that the OVRA would not leave protection. Perhaps the guards are asleep in one of the other trucks. But that makes no sense. A guard found sleeping while on duty in a conflict situation is charged with a general court-martial offense in all Western armies."

They crawled closer and closer in the tall grass. *Surely, by now, guards would have heard or seen them.* Walter rose and helped Sofia rise. "Let's make an old-fashioned charge. Shoot first and ask questions later. Deal?"

"Deal."

Spread a hundred yards apart, the pair advanced quickly, circle the trucks, and checked the cabs and passenger areas, but found no one.

"Listen, Sofia. Quiet!" They heard the barely audible, constant hum of a generator and radio static. Walter put his index finger to his lips and whispered, "There's someone in that radio truck. Probably relaying communications from those troops to OVRA headquarters."

Sofia jerked the door open and spotted a young soldier at a massive radio suite. She pointed her submachine gun at the lad and commanded, "*Mani in alto, operatere radio!*"

Caught utterly by surprise, the lad swirled around in his chair, raised his hands high, and squawked loudly, "*Mi arrende. Per favore, no me fucilare*—do not shoot me."

Walter jumped into the radio truck, disarmed the lad, and indicated for him to exit. Walter stripped off the lad's jacket and motioned for him to unbutton his shirt. "Sofia, here is a chance for you to get out of that blood-splashed jacket. Put on his clothes." Walter trussed up the radio operator tightly with their climbing rope, covered his mouth with adhesive tape, and eased him to the ground.

Sofia kicked him softly on the shoulder and said in Italian, "Send a prayer to your patron saint that you will live to see tomorrow's light. Make no attempt to undo your bindings. When your comrades return they will rescue you. *Comprendere?*"

The soldier nodded in understanding.

Walter searched the four remaining trucks, found an officer's lightweight coat, and slipped it on.

He turned to Sofia. "Reckon we can pass for OVRA soldiers for a few seconds? That's all we'll need."

She looked at him quizzically but made no comment.

"I'll explain when we're on the road." He released the safety on his submachine gun and motioned for Sofia to do the same. "We've got to disable these trucks and radio gear so they can't follow us or radio for help. Let's start on that far truck and work our way back to this command truck."

With methodical precision, the pair shot out all the trucks' tires and blasted out their radiators. Walter found pliers in one of the trucks' toolboxes and, for insurance, snipped all the trucks' spark-plug wires. He opened the door to the radio cab and emptied a full magazine into the equipment: Sparks flew as vacuum tubes and all manner of electronic equipment erupted into the cab. He commented with a satisfied grin, "We have effectively isolated those soldiers for a day or so when they return. It is a respectable hike to the main road—perhaps twenty miles."

They climbed into the cab of the command truck. The key was in the ignition. Walter started the engine, put the car in drive, and they accelerated toward the main highway.

chapter seventeen

In the Rendakom Mountains, Eritrea. 8 September 1937.

The staccato of Walter's and Sofia's submachine gunfire echoed loudly back and forth between the granite walls of the ravine. Though faint, *Colonnello* Visco recognized immediately the familiar sound of the Beretta MAB-38 submachine gun. A ripple of fear and concern raced through his body. *What is happening? Who is firing those machine guns?* "Halt!" He commanded his detail of alpine troops. His mind raced for an explanation. *It can't be those spies. They are ahead of us and will probably try an ambush as we close the gap. Perhaps it is a raid by those Muslim rebels. But it's not likely this side of the mountains. It must be that the guards have gone berserk. I will have them all standing before a court martial.* "*Capitano* Dante Caito, come forward."

"*Si, Colonnello.*"

"You heard?"

"*Si, Colonnello.*"

"Your explanation."

"*Mi Colonnello,* I have none. It is a mystery."

"Why would your guards be firing so vigorously?"

"*Scuso mi, Colonnello.* I did not post guards. The radio operator in the command truck is the only one there. I don't know who is firing."

"*Voi grullo cretin!*" spouted the Colonel in an uncontrolled rage. He slapped the Captain with all his might.

Capitano Dante Caito staggered back two steps. He recovered and snapped a proper salute. "*Scuso mi, Colonnello*. I thought I heard you say, 'Bring all your troops.' It is my error."

"*Si!* Take a squad and in double time return to our trucks and radio me what you find." He composed himself. "If all is well, drive our trucks to Asmera and over the mountain pass to Mits'iwa on the sea. We do not know where this mountain trail exits on the east side of the mountains. Search for us. Move!"

∽

Walter and Sofia were traveling almost due north on the main highway about ten miles south of Asmera in the OVRA command truck. Sofia tied her hair in a tight bun on the back of her neck and wore the radio operator's pith helmet. Under brief observation, she could easily pass as a young OVRA soldier. Walter, in his OVRA officer's jacket, completed their disguise. They had gone through Decamere an hour earlier without incident. They had even received a snappy salute from two OVRA soldiers in front of the city's telecommunications building.

"We'll be driving through Asmera in a few minutes. I don't expect problems if we maintain our façade, which has served us well so far." Walter slowed the command truck as they approached the outskirts of the Alpine city. "Keep your machine gun handy. Use it only as a last resort. The last thing we need is to attract attention."

"I understand." Sofia loaded a fresh magazine, cycled the bolt, and snapped the safety to FUOCO. She cradled the weapon on her lap.

Walter drove carefully, and noticed that any time citizens saw an officer in an OVRA command truck, they showed curious fear. Near the town's center, the highway turned east. Just a few miles ahead, the Rendakom Mountains rose in front of them. Fortunately, no one had dared to challenge them. When they were about to exit the city on its east side, Walter cautioned, "At the base of the mountains we can expect a serious roadblock. This highway is the only passageway over those mountains, and it is the gateway to the Red Sea."

"Well and good, Texan, but what happens if we get past that roadblock? How do we escape this OVRA-controlled, Italian-Army-occupied province? I'm not about to swim across that shark-infested Red Sea." She sat up straight and adjusted the pith helmet lower on her forehead. "And how long will it be before the OVRA will pick up our trail? Level with me, Walter Gregory. What devious plan have you and your iniquitous intelligence confederates concocted to bid this country *arrivederci, au revoir, auf wiedersehen, do svidaniya,* goodbye?"

"With good fortune, and your saints looking out for us, we will arrive at our rendezvous point tomorrow afternoon. Then it is *adios,* Abyssinia."

"That's cute, Walter, but I need more information." Sofia snapped. "Stop being coy with me. I'm a grown woman."

"Indeed you are, *Signora.* Indeed you are." A flamboyant Walter responded. "Fair question, *paisano.* I will answer when we get closer to our escape point."

He waited several seconds before he spoke again. "I haven't revealed the complete getaway plan because it is dangerous, and I didn't want to add to your worries. If you were captured, you wouldn't be able to withstand constant torture for very long. To ease the excruciating pain, you, as most everyone else, would tell your interrogators what they want to know. Should that happen, several key intelligence agents would be thrust into mortal danger, the MI6 would lose valuable contacts here, and the escape route would be compromised for others, both into and out of this country."

Sofia reflected on Walter's comments for a few seconds. "Thanks for the explanation. I understand and won't bother you again about it."

The command truck left the city and the highway began its gentle climb to the base of the mountains. A couple of miles ahead, Walter spotted the expected roadblock. He began to slow the command truck.

"What's our strategy? Crash it? Bluff our way through, or shoot it out, and 'Katy, bar the door'?" Sofia quizzed.

"It's a little of all those options." Walter saw that the guards had parked a large truck across the road and that there were about six soldiers manning a roadblock. The right side of the road was chocka-block next to the granite mountain. On the left was a sharp drop into a gully several dozen feet below. It was an ideal position for this roadblock.

"I'll drive close to that truck and try to bluff our way across." He gently applied the brakes and the command truck slowed. Two guards on each side of the car approached with their submachine guns slung over their shoulders, obviously not expecting trouble from those in this OVRA command vehicle.

Walter instructed, "Roll your window down, and open fire when I say, or if you see that our bluff fails. We will have to kill all of them. *Capisci?*"

"I don't like it, Walter. But I understand. Count on me."

"I am."

Walter stopped the car about ten feet from the blocking truck, and rolled down his window as the first guard on his side approached. Walter looked at him with quiet disdain. The soldier snapped to attention and saluted his senior officer.

"*Scuso mi, Capitano,* I must ask for your papers. It is the order from OVRA headquarters."

Walter replied in Italian, "Of course, *Sergente.* Unfortunately, they are in my dress coat at the foot of a gully in the Rendakom Mountains." He pointed to Sofia. "While I was hiking with *Colonnello* Visco to find those two spies, he ordered me to return to our trucks on the double time and drive this radio operator to his new command base at Mits'iwa. In the haste, confusion, and the need to obey this command with dispatch, I failed to bring my dress jacket." Walter paused for effect and smiled weakly. "I am sure you understand."

With his left eyebrow cocked, the Sergeant asked, "Your name, please, *Capitano*."

"I am *Capitano* Dante Caito, Communications Officer on *Colonnello* Visco's staff. Move that truck, I need to pass."

The sergeant began to swing his Beretta MAB-38 forward. He shouted loudly, "You are an imposter. The spy! *Capitano* Dante Caito is my commanding officer."

"Sofia, fire!" In an instant, her submachine gun began to chatter and 38-caliber bullets ripped into the two guards on her side. Blood spattered on the car as the soldiers were thrown lifeless to the ground.

Walter's 38 six-shooter had spoken twice and the sergeant fell backwards with two spouting holes in his throat.

The soldier in the guard shack on Sofia's side heard the ruckus and ran onto the road. In an instant, he surveyed the scene, lifted his rifle, and fired. The windshield next to Sofia splattered into thousands of miniature shards. Sofia, her face and arms covered with blood from dozens of small tears, leaped from the car and charged the soldier. He was dumfounded for an instant when he saw that a madwoman with a submachine gun was attacking him. That hesitation cost him his life. Sofia riddled him with a dozen bullets.

The third guard on Walter's side raised his rifle and aimed it at him. Before the guard could pull the trigger, two 38-caliber bullets from Walter's six-shooter caught him square in the chest. He was dead before he hit the ground.

The quiet was startling. Walter, a little shaken, went to the downed soldiers on his side of the car and retrieved their magazines. To relieve his stress, which he knew was also enveloping Sofia, he shouted, "Nice shooting, pardner'. Well done."

She was sitting on the road, shaking, and dripping blood from her numerous cuts. She began to insert another magazine into her submachine gun, and shouted with a touch of hysteria, "To hell with you, Walter Gregory. What have you made me?" She began to pull some of the glass shards from her right arm. "I'm a cold-blooded killer."

He rushed to her. "My God, Sofia. Any glass in your eyes?"

"No. The pith helmet took most of those shards."

He knelt next to her and carefully inspected her face and arms. "I see lots of small cuts on your face and a few shards in your arm."

He went into the guard shack and found several canteens of water. He returned and wiped the blood from Sofia's face, then kissed her cheek and said, "I'll help with those glass shards—but later. When we get to Mits'iwa we'll stop and get iodine and dressing for those wounds. Now, we need to get out of here fast. Can you help me move that truck blocking the road?"

"Yes. I'm okay." With Walter's help she rose, picked up her sub-machine gun, and tossed it into the truck. "Let's go."

Walter checked—there was no key in the ignition. It was probably in one of the guard's pockets. He put the car's gearshift in neutral, straightened the wheels, and released the emergency brake. "Let's push this monster over the edge into that gully."

The truck moved forward and gained momentum, slowly at first, and then at an accelerated pace. The pair fell away and the truck leaped off the cliff and crashed into hundreds of pieces as it tumbled down the granite slope and finally came to rest at the bottom of the gully.

"Thanks, pal."

Still shaken, Sofia could manage only, "Okay."

Walter picked up the magazines from the fallen soldiers who Sofia had killed. "You'll probably need these later. We're a long way from an Allied country and freedom. When the OVRA agents in Asmera find this carnage, they will know we have transportation, and where we are headed. At least *Colonnello* Visco is neutralized for a while."

Almost on cue, two Fiat CR-32 scout planes flew over the pass at a low altitude. "No doubt, they're looking for us," Walter quipped.

Feeling somewhat better, Sofia commented lamely, "Let's get out of this place. I'll ride shotgun pardner."

She used her pith helmet to sweep away the glass shards on the truck's seat. Then she climbed into the car, placed her head back on her seat, closed her eyes, and said, "I'm sorry for what I said, Walter. I have a difficult time handling the stress of these killings—it's not in my nature. I understand it's a matter of self-preservation, but it's repulsive. I've had my fill of it. I pray to Saint Sophia to save me from more of these murderous confrontations." Sofia worked to remove the shards from her arms and mop the blood.

Walter started the command truck, put it in gear, and released the clutch. The car moved forward and in a few seconds Walter had it moving on the twisting mountain road, headed for the summit about seven miles away.

chapter eighteen

Mits'iwa on the Red Sea. 8 September 1937.

Sofia's vigor was restored during the forty-five minute drive over the scenic mountain road.

Just before the pair entered the small town of Mits'iwa, Walter pulled off the road and parked the truck under the shade of a large myrtle tree. The fresh breeze from the Red Sea hinted that they were close to their escape. Walter checked Sofia's facial wounds. "We need to take care of those cuts."

"Okay, *paisano.*"

He saw fresh blood on the left sleeve of Sofia's shirt. "Let's look at that arm. Roll up your sleeve, pardner." After an intense look, he said, "Several of those cuts on your arm are deeper than we first thought." He drew his hunting knife from his backpack, cut her sleeve away, and used it to wrap her arm.

"I didn't know you were also a medical doctor, Texan."

"This is no joke, Sofia. We have to get you disinfectant and bandages. Infection in even a small cut is all too common in this area. That scratch on my leg needs attention also. It's begun to fester."

Walter exited the car and shed his officer's jacket. "Sofia, get rid of that uniform. I don't reckon OVRA officials would receive a jolly reception in this Muslim enclave. Let's be civilians again. It's time for you to return to your ol' sweet self."

She managed a half laugh at the absurdity of Walter's statement. "Just call me 'Machine-gun Sofia,' the mob moll from Asmera." She shed the OVRA jacket and shirt.

Walter retrieved a shovel from the toolbox, took the uniforms, and walked a hundred yards towards the sea. He returned in a few minutes and said, "Those uniforms are buried and won't be found for a long time, if ever."

He entered the truck, started it, and eased onto the roadway, headed north. "By tomorrow morning, at the latest, the OVRA will be in force over that summit scouring this area for us. Then there's *Colonnello* Visco and his squad. I reckon that by tomorrow afternoon they'll exit that mountain trail somewhere below here. We'll be trapped between these two OVRA forces that are committed to obliterating us." He shifted into fourth gear and the truck purred smoothly.

"Walter, you draw a grim future for us. I don't want the details, but I trust that Allied intelligence and you have developed contingency options. True?"

"True!"

Walter drove the command car into Mits'iwa and stopped the truck in an alley next to the general store. "I'm going inside to check for medical supplies. Stay in the truck and behave! I'll be back shortly."

"Yes. I understand. I'll be okay."

Walter entered the small store and spotted the international symbol for apothecary—the mortar and pestle, which hung over a counter in the rear of the shop. Behind it were two shelves with a few bottles and some small boxes.

The proprietor immediately recognized Walter as the spy for whom the OVRA was searching. He greeted Walter with a resounding, "*Ahian wa sahian*—welcome to my store. How may I be of service?"

"Good afternoon, sir," Walter responded formally. "Do you have iodine, sterile bandages, and adhesive tape in stock?"

The proprietor smiled broadly and said, "Today, you are in luck. These items are on my shelf. Where is your wound? Perhaps I can help."

Walter wanted to keep this transaction as short as possible. He got to the point. "It's my leg. A cut is infected. I can take care of it."

"No. No. I insist. It is my moral obligation to help strangers in need. Let me see your wound."

Not wanting to create a ruckus, Walter pulled up his right trouser leg. "I cut it on a granite outcropping in the mountains yesterday."

The proprietor carefully inspected the wound. "Indeed, it is seriously infected. I will call my wife. She is a nurse at our clinic. She can help."

Walter, anxious to return to Sofia and get away, snapped, "Not necessary, I have to leave. Please sell me the supplies I've asked for."

"Let me introduce myself. I am Kateb Fudial, the proprietor of this establishment. And you are?"

"The medicine, please. I must leave." Walter said impatiently.

Fudial raised an eyebrow. "Stranger, tell me who you are and why you are in this miserable little town during the Italian occupation." Fudial did not wait for an answer. "You are not a tourist, and you are not an Italian. The fascists wear uniforms, travel in groups, and are well armed." He carefully weighed his next comment. "You are the American, Walter Gregory, who is escaping from the OVRA."

Walter's eyes narrowed at Fudial's startling statement and his right hand moved to his holstered Smith and Wesson 38 six-shooter. "How do you know?"

"Your picture is on posters about the town, and so is your partner's, Sofia Russo." Fudial cracked a small smile. "The OVRA is efficient in its communication skills." He pointed to a small radio on the counter. "And the radio constantly broadcasts your descriptions and your crimes against the Italians."

Walter drew his Smith and Wesson 38. "Hand me those medical supplies and I leave here without trouble."

Fudial smiled broadly and extended his hand in friendship. "Mister Gregory, welcome to my establishment. Anyone fleeing from the OVRA is a friend of mine—most especially for spying on the Italians. We have no love for those devils here in Eritrea." He could not conceal his anger. "Those thugs shot down my brother and my nephew in cold blood right in front of my store, and for no reason other than that they were Arabs and Muslims."

Walter slowly returned his Smith and Wesson 38 to his holster. He was at a loss for words. He paused for a few seconds to appraise the scene. His best option for making his rendezvous and escape with Sofia from Abyssinia was to be straightforward with Fudial. "You are correct. Madame Russo and I are escaping from the Italian secret police. Unfortunately, she has several cuts on her face and arms that need attention. An OVRA bullet shattered our windshield and glass shards ripped into her. So far, we've been careful and aggressive, and Lady Luck has been on our side. By tomorrow, OVRA soldiers *en masse* will flood into this area, and another group will be through a mountain pass to the south of here."

"Indeed," Fudial commented. "We'll address those problems later. Now, bring in Madame Russo."

Fudial welcomed Sofia, and without ado, said, "You two, follow me to my apartment in the back. My wife, a nurse, is best qualified to tend to both of you."

Fudial made no introduction and spoke in Arabic to his wife, who was clad in the traditional abaya. She smiled, embarrassed, at this unfamiliar and awkward situation. She inspected the wounds on Sofia's face, cleaned them with alcohol, swabbed them with iodine, and put bandages on only three of the deepest cuts.

To ease Sofia's stress, Walter commented with a mocking voice, "My, my, pardner, you look just like an Apache Indian in war paint, ready to go on a raiding party. Who are you after?"

Sofia smiled and said, "You! You land-grabbing Texan. I'm gonna get you. Come here and kiss me to make my face well."

Walter pecked her cheek, uncertain how much affection he should display in front of his new Muslim patrons.

"You know better than that! Kiss me, damn you, like you mean it."

Walter kissed Sofia full on the mouth.

Fudial's wife covered her face with her hands at this openly sexual gesture. But she smiled inwardly as she saw the love between the two strangers. She took Sofia's arm and inspected it closely. She emitted a small gasp and indicated, with hand motions, that several cuts needed to be stitched closed. She carefully and gently moved across the cuts with her fingers, checking to see if any of the glass shards remained. She found two small pieces and deftly removed them with tweezers. Then, with her eyes and body signals, she asked permission to proceed.

Sofia nodded her approval. Walter held Sofia's hand as the nurse proceeded. About twenty minutes later, Sofia had her left arm dressed in five places with thick wraps of gauze and adhesive tape. The nurse rigged a sling to keep Sofia's left arm high across her chest.

Fudial told Sofia that her arm must be kept high for a day or so to prevent oozing and infection.

Fudial's wife motioned for Walter to sit. He pulled up his right trouser leg. After she looked at his wound, she shook her head sideways, communicating that the wound was seriously infected. She showed Walter a surgical knife and indicated that she should lance and drain the wound.

Knowing that this procedure needed to be done, Walter nodded affirmatively. Afterwards, the nurse swabbed the wound with iodine, wrapped it in gauze, and indicated he must apply iodine three times daily, as well as fresh bandages.

Walter shook Fudial's hand, nodded to his wife in thanks, and offered the couple a thousand-dollar gold certificate.

Fudial refused and said, "My friend, Mister Gregory, it is my moral obligation to offer succor to strangers. I ask that, in return, one day you do a personal favor for a stranger." Then, with a crooked smile he said, "Besides, I am fulfilled that in some small way I may have defied the OVRA."

Walter said humbly, "Fair enough. You have my word."

He helped Sofia rise and then snapped a salute to Fudial and his wife and bowed his head slightly. "Thank you and best of luck. We are taking our leave." He and Sofia started walking towards the door.

Fudial said, "My friends, please wait. Your escape scenario is just beginning. You are in serious trouble. Without my help, you will be in the OVRA's hands by tomorrow afternoon at the latest. It will be dark soon. You and the woman will remain here tonight." Walter and Sofia knew that Fudial was correct. Trapped between two OVRA forces, they had little chance of escape. The truck, their clothes, and overall appearance gave them away, a danger which was heightened by the area-wide saturation of their descriptions. "You are correct, my friend." Realizing that he had no other choice, Walter reluctantly revealed the next step in their escape plan. "Can you arrange transportation for us? We need to go south down the coast to meet our contact."

"Where are you going?"

"Best you don't know."

"Yes. That is okay. Tomorrow, my older son will take you south in our wagon. Our horse is old, but she still has lots of life."

"We've got to get rid of that OVRA command truck."

"Easily done. In a few minutes, I will have my youngest son drive it over that dirt trail that heads north for several miles and leave it at a small cove. When the OVRA discover it, perhaps they will believe that you escaped by dhow from there. This maneuver will keep the OVRA busy for a few hours. And I will caution my son to erase his tracks as he returns."

"Will he be safe?"

"Of course. He knows that area well and has friends there."

"Please ask your son to disable that truck and to snip the spark-plug wires, smash the radiator, and if he has the time, drain the oil from the engine."

"That he will do."

"Thank you."

"Unfortunately, we have no spare room for you two. My other son will fix a place for you in our wagon in the barn. He will arrange straw on the wagon bed, cover it with a blanket, and leave a blanket for you to cover yourselves. It will be chilly this evening. Our old horse will not bother you too much."

The pair, tired, hungry, and malodorous, were warmly ensconced in their welcome quarters in the barn as they reviewed the day's events. Walter checked their backpacks to ensure that all was in place. Fudial's wife brought the pair a thick and tasty soup of unknown ingredients, with wheat bread and warm tea. Sofia thought the fare was a repast fit for royalty.

When they had completed their meal, Walter pulled up the blanket and kissed Sofia lightly. They slept deeply in each other's arms.

ా

Immediately after sunrise, Fudial's oldest son, Shazeb, awoke the pair and offered them thick coffee and buttered bread. He gave them a few minutes to complete their breakfast. Then he said, "My father has sent you these clothes, which are more fitting for this area. Most of the Arabs wear similar garb. It would be nonsense for you to travel in your Western clothing."

As the couple changed clothing, Shazeb loaded two baskets of food and water onto the wagon under the seat. When the pair emerged in their Arabic disguises, he said to Walter, "Help me put these melons into the wagon. We must have a cargo to curb suspicions." When the task was completed, he asked, "Tell me, where are we going?"

Walter responded, "It would be best if you didn't know."

"I understand."

"However, I will say that my rendezvous is quite a few miles south of here. According to my map, I see that the road is not paved. What kind of a road is it?"

The son put the tack on his horse and said, "It's an old camel trail, deeply rutted in places, rough in spots, but generally it is fairly even." He finished getting his horse ready. "Time to go."

"Wait a minute," Walter commented. "We are deeply grateful to your family for your bravery and generous help; I'm compelled to return a favor." Walter withdrew a thousand-dollar gold certificate from his money belt and offered it to Shazeb. "Please accept this bill. Not as payment, but as a token of our gratitude to your family."

With sincere humility, Shazeb responded, "What can my family do with such a large gold certificate in this poor, Italian-occupied country? Should I try, the OVRA would immediately arrest me and question me harshly. I would break under torture and tell them all about you. My family would be threatened. No, American, I cannot accept your money, however sincerely offered. What my family does is done for Allah, and to rid our province of the Italians."

Shazeb hopped into the seat and guided the horse to turn the wagon around. "Sir, you sit here with me on the seat. Madame, you sit on the wagon's bed with your back to the seat, and arrange the melons around you."

Walter tossed the two backpacks onto the bed of the wagon next to Sofia, covered them with a ragged tarpaulin, and scattered melons over them. He climbed into the seat.

Shazeb snapped the reins and the wagon moved slowly ahead.

ℰ⁀ꝺ

That afternoon, OVRA soldiers stormed into Fudial's store. The squad leader questioned the shop owner, asking whether he knew anything about the two escaped spies—an American man and an Italian woman.

Fudial, in fear mixed with a hint of anguish, responded with a straight face, "No, of course not. What do I have to do with spies?"

The OVRA soldiers began to search the store and his living quarters. One of the soldiers found the torn and bloody OVRA shirtsleeve and discarded bloody gauze that his wife had tossed carelessly into a waste bin. The squad leader demanded that Fudial explain this culpable evidence.

Not skilled in subterfuge, Fudial stumbled and gave an inept response.

The squad leader dangled the torn OVRA shirtsleeve in front of Fudial. "One of the spies is wounded? Which? Tell me. Where are those spies?"

Fudial remained silent with an indolent stare.

"I know that the spies were here and you helped them. Tell me truthfully," the squad leader demanded.

Fudial, totally flustered and afraid, responded, "I do not know anything about spies."

"You're a liar and a rebel!" cried the squad leader. He hoisted his Beretta submachine gun to the firing position and clicked off the safety. "Last chance."

Fudial remained defiantly silent.

The OVRA soldier squeezed the trigger and a volley of 38 caliber bullets ripped into Fudial. His wife ran to her husband. Another volley cut her down.

chapter nineteen

Arafali, Eritrea, Abyssinia. 9 September 1937.

The wagon bounced along the dirt road to Arafali. Sofia was tossed about and did her best to offset the jarring by holding tightly to the sides of the wagon.

Walter had an easier time of it. He sat on a spring-balanced seat and only had to absorb an occasional jolt during the daylong trip. They were able to blend in with other travelers: wagons filled with produce and a small camel caravan. Their pace was slow as the wagon made its way along the narrow road. Goatherds moved their flocks toward the mountains.

Throughout the day, *Regia Aeronautica Italiana* aircraft flew patrols over the area, no doubt looking for the two spies. Their ruse was working, as the aviators apparently did not spot anything suspicious. Walter observed that none of the aircraft changed course or altitude for a second look. Apparently, all the movement along this byway looked normal.

Walter reckoned that by now the OVRA had found the abandoned command truck by that small cove. From the increased aircraft activity later in the day, it seemed likely the OVRA had not taken the bait and believed that he and Sofia had escaped by boat.

By mid-afternoon, Sofia had had enough. "Walter, tell Shazeb to stop this torture wagon. My *derrière* must be black and blue from the pounding." She smiled tauntingly. "And don't get any smart ideas, or else I will slug you where it hurts, but not too hard. I've got to get out of this contraption to stretch and massage where it hurts. I need water and victuals if I'm going to survive this endless, agonizing trek into oblivion. And I need a hug to refresh my resolve."

After a half-hour respite, Walter said urgently, "Let's go. We must get to Arafali before nightfall."

"You are a damn slave driver, Walter Gregory. Why? What's the hurry?" She thought about it and concluded that Walter most likely had arranged a rendezvous with a captain of a dhow who would sail them out of Eritrea tonight. "Fess up, Walter. Don't keep me guessing."

"Not yet Sofia. We're still in danger. *Colonnello* Visco is ahead of us."

Sofia snapped, "What time do we sail?"

Walter gave her a crooked smile and said, "Your deduction is on target."

"Come here, Walter, and give me another hug. I will need it to tolerate my suffering ahead."

❧

Near dusk, the wagon entered Arafali—a small fishing village on an inconsequential cove located deep between two long promontories that projected into the Mits'iwa Channel on the Red Sea. For all practical purposes, Arafali was hidden from maritime traffic.

Shortly after they entered the village, two masked and armed rebel fighters seemed to appear out of nowhere. They demanded the driver stop the wagon. "Who are you? And where are you from? We do not know you." They leveled their Beretta model 38 submachine guns at the trio. "Get down!"

Complying with their orders, Walter and Shazeb scrambled down from the high seat. Sofia hopped off the wagon, causing several melons to cascade to the ground and smash open. The trio stood in a line.

Shazeb explained who they were, and where they were from. Walter told them that he was in Arafali to meet the sailor Aamir Sanawbar.

"Why?" snapped the lead guard. "What concern do you have with Sanawbar?"

Walter responded in a deep, steady, businesslike voice, "I'm not at liberty to say. Ask him."

"Why are you and the woman dressed as Arabs?"

"Ask Sanawbar."

Sofia remained mute and wondered if this scene was sincere or just theatre to impress the fugitives.

The lead guard finally said, "Then it is true, you are the two spies hunted by the OVRA. They are offering a handsome reward. Not so?"

Walter nodded.

"Pass, friend. Sanawbar is at the dock just ahead preparing his dhow for another smuggling run. You must be his contraband." Both guards started to laugh at the humor of the situation.

Walter and Sofia said goodbye to Shazeb. He turned his wagon around and headed north towards his village and family—unaware of the horror that awaited him. Walter spotted the dock several hundred feet ahead. Alongside was a huge sambuk dhow with two large triangular sails.

Sanawbar saw the pair walking toward his boat and beckoned them to come aboard. "Welcome to your new home for the next few days. Look around. Inspect your sleeping quarters. Impressive, no?"

After the introductions, Walter and Sofia followed Sanawbar as he guided them around the boat. The fetid odor of decaying fish caused the pair to turn green with roiling stomachs.

"Walter, you are insane if you think I am going to spend three days on this garbage scow," cried Sofia. "I'm ill!" she spat. She sat on a nearby stool and took a swath of cloth from her loose sleeve and held it in front of her nose.

"Your choice, my lady fair, this scow or the OVRA."

"Damn you, Walter Gregory." She grabbed him and pulled him down to her. "Here's another fine, stinking mess you've gotten me into." She flashed a faux smile.

Sanawbar interceded. "My dear *Signora*, your nose will become accustomed in no time." He smiled mischievously. "Frankly, I culture this putrid odor to keep the unwanted away from my dhow—I can run my business, some say illegal business, without too many interruptions, especially from the Italian Navy."

"What's your plan?" Walter demanded.

"Of course, Mister Gregory. I know who you are from the OVRA radio announcements." He paused to take a deep drag on his Turkish cigarette. "British intelligence has commissioned me to take you to Aden, their Crown Colony on the tip of the Arabian coast." He looked coldly at Sofia. "MI6 made no mention about a woman. They will have to pay extra if I get both of you to Aden alive and unharmed."

Miffed that Sanawbar was so mercenary, Walter snapped, "You'll get your blood money."

"Mister Gregory, there is no need for anger. I am but a simple sailor eking out a meager living in this miserable Italian occupation."

"My apologies, Sanawbar." *Meager, indeed!* "Let's shove off."

"We'll sail after dusk. I will use my inboard marine engine to propel my boat out of this cove. By the time we reach the Mits'iwa Channel it will be dark and we will unfurl the sails. With favorable winds, it will take three days sailing to reach British Aden. It is about three hundred miles south of here on the Arabian Peninsula."

"That checks with my briefing."

"Finally, Walter. The truth will out," Sofia sniped.

Sanawbar tossed the cigarette overboard. "I am surprised to see that you came from Mits'iwa. British intelligence told me that you would enter Eritrea by that old goat trail in the mountains about a half-mile up the road."

"We had troubles with the OVRA on our tail, so we took a roundabout way to get here."

Sanawbar grabbed Walter's arm. "Are you saying that an OVRA troop is on that goat trail and headed here? Tell me the truth!" Sanawbar was agitated. "I've had scouts posted on the trail for the last two days waiting to notify me when they spotted you, and to guide you here. They have not reported."

"Two days ago, we saw *Colonnello* Visco leading a squad of well-armed alpine troops over that trail headed toward the summit. He ought to arrive on this side of the mountains almost any time."

Sanawbar shouted, "Are you saying that *Colonnello* Visco, the OVRA leader, is in this area? You are certain? This is the *Colonnello* who bombed our villages, ordered his Black Shirt troops to murder our people and rape our women, and this is the man who committed blasphemy by desecrating the Holy Koran and disparaging the Prophet!"

Walter shook his head and said, "Visco and his squad should be within a few miles of this side of the mountains by now. We should shove off before he gets here. Let's get underway."

"No!" After a moment, Sanawbar calmed and spat into the bay. "My people cannot afford to have him and his thugs in this area." On a moment's reflection, he said, "Actually, I would be most pleased to meet the esteemed *Colonnello* and for him to enjoy my hospitality." He drew a submachine gun from under a table in the wheelhouse. "We know that goat trail well. I will send our fighters to alert my men waiting for you to ambush the Italian occupiers and to make sure that *Colonnello* Visco is unharmed. Will you join us?"

Walter was incensed. He spun around to face Sanawbar and responded angrily to his plan to eliminate the squad. "God, no! We have had enough killing. No more. Take the soldiers prisoner."

"American, I am in charge here," Sanawbar said with a firm voice. "We cannot afford to have OVRA soldiers on this side of the mountains." His black eyes flashed, "What am I to do with OVRA prisoners-feed them, house them, and tend to their needs? No. It is not reasonable." He cycled the bolt on his weapon to chamber a round. "You understand."

Sofia looked haggard from grief. She was weary but defiant. "No, I don't understand." She rose, sat next to Walter, and nuzzled against his face and arms.

☙

Sustained gunfire echoed down the canyon and flooded the area. Sofia grabbed Walter and mumbled, "They did it. Sanawbar has killed those Italian soldiers." She drew her handkerchief and wiped tears away from her eyes. "What sort of a savage is that madman? And he is supposed to save us?" She asked rhetorically, "Walter, when, please tell me, when will we be through with blackguards and become civilized again?

Sanawbar climbed aboard his dhow and his first mate pushed the bound *Colonnello* Visco onto the quarterdeck. "Welcome to my home, such as it is, *Colonnello*. I shall make it a point that your stay, however short, is meaningful."

Visco spotted Sofia and there was fear in his eyes. "*Signora* Russo, what do these fellows plan for me?" he asked in a hollow voice.

Sofia stared at Visco and hate flared in her eyes. With a reckless twist to her mouth, she raged at him, "I do not know. And I do not give a damn."

His eyes became vague and empty. "You are an Italian and my countryman. Please, intercede for me."

Sofia focused blazing eyes on *Colonnello* Visco. Her voice was dry, cool, and sardonic. "I am proud to say that I killed several of your OVRA fascist thugs who were hindering our escape. I am ashamed that they were my countrymen. I would also kill you, except these fishermen have priority."

Sanawbar told the pair, "Get inside the wheel house and close the door. I have to entertain our guest."

A few minutes later, Walter and Sofia heard terrifying screams and a large splash. Sofia gasped and grabbed Walter's hand. Almost immediately, they heard Sanawbar shouting to his crew, "Cast off the forward line." A second later, "Cast off the aft line."

Sanawbar entered the wheelhouse and hit the starter of his finely tuned Marine-Packard engine and it roared to life. He swung the wheel to starboard, and the dhow slipped slowly into the Mits'iwa Channel.

chapter twenty

On the Red Sea, en route to Aden. 10 September 1937.

Early in the morning, the moon was full and its light reflected in a frenzied pattern on the gently rolling sea. The dhow's sails were fully rigged and the ship was cruising at about twelve knots. Walter and Sofia, for the first time in many days, had nothing to do: no pressing escapes to plan; no OVRA soldiers to avoid; no careful schemes to concoct. They were bored. They had run out of conversation, and knew any romance would be inappropriate. Besides, they were too mentally and physically exhausted to do much of anything except sit and watch the birds fly by, and watch the other dhows, of all makes and sizes, crisscrossing the water. Most of their energy was spent trying to tolerate the nauseating stench emanating from the bilge.

Just before dawn, an Italian motor torpedo boat (MTB), MAS-568, hailed Sanawbar's dhow with flashing red lights, a siren, and a powerful spotlight. The international maritime signals communicated, "Heave to. Authorities want to board you." Shortly, the Italian craft corrected its course to intersect the dhow.

Sanawbar had been operating with full sails and his inboard engine purring in idle. He cut his engine, and ordered his first mate to have the crew furl the sails and prepare for a boarding party.

Walter and Sofia saw that the Italian Navy was about to board and search the dhow; they wondered what plan Sanawbar had devised to keep them safe. "It's okay, Sofia. This ol' smuggler has survived many inspections before. He is shrewd enough not to be caught with two OVRA-wanted 'spies' on board."

Sofia snuggled next to Walter and said with a small, ominous laugh, "I hope you're correct. After all we've been through these past few days, and this close to approaching our safe haven, I would abhor being captured now." With steely determination, and finality in her eyes, she implored, "Have your pistol ready and do as you promised me."

"Sofia, relax." He gently took her in his arms. "Sanawbar will protect us. It is to his advantage to keep us safe. British intelligence will reward him handsomely when he gets us unharmed to Aden."

"That may be so." Tears sprang into her eyes. "I don't understand your tangled schemes. But if you have affection for me, you will do what you promised." She kissed him lightly. "I'm counting on it, *caro amico*."

The Italian MTB was about one hundred yards to starboard and approaching steadily. Sanawbar snapped open a trap door to the bilge. It was located under the deck and held his catch of old, fetid rock-skipper fish. He commanded Walter and Sofia, "Hurry. Get below. Take your backpacks." The pair complied quickly and without comment. Ensconced in the putrid bilge, Walter ensured that the shards with radioactive dust and the poison-gas canisters were intact.

Sanawbar returned to the deck to greet the Italians. Meanwhile, several of his crew dumped decaying fish on top of the pair to ensure that the fastidious Italian naval officer would decide not to carefully search the stinking bilge. He cut the idling engine and told his first mate to stand by on the lines.

Capitano di Corvetta Nazario Tomaino had patrolled these waters for many months and knew most of the legitimate fishermen. He also knew that Sanawbar was probably a smuggler, carrying contraband. Unfortunately, neither he nor any of the other patrol captains could find evidence against Sanawbar. On this morning, Tomaino was looking for the two escaped spies: Walter Gregory, the

American agent, and Sofia Savoy Russo, the Italian traitor. Evidence indicated that these two murderers were at sea and headed for the closest Allied-held territory in the region: either Aden, the British Crown Colony, or Djibouti, in the French Territory of the Afars and Issas.

The chief boatswain on the MTB hailed the dhow. "Stand by. A boarding party is coming aboard."

Lines across, the Italian boat was snug against Sanawbar's dhow. He shouted to the Italian captain, "You are welcome. Come aboard and bring some of your steaming pasta; my crew longs for its delicious taste."

Capitano di Corvetta Nazario Tomaino and three of his Marines leaped aboard the dhow with their Beretta 38s drawn.

Sanawbar grabbed the captain's hand and shook it vigorously. "I'm delighted to see you again, *Capitano* Tomaino. It has been several weeks since we met last. You are well? Capturing lots of smugglers, I presume?" He gestured to a bench atop the fish catch. "Please sit and have a cup of tea with me."

"Shut up, Sanawbar. This is not a social call and you know it," the captain snapped. He waved his pistol at Sanawbar and stated, "You are a smuggler and worse, and I am going to prove it. *Comprendere?*"

"*Si. Si, Capitano.* But, I am just a fisherman, eking out a living in these troubled times." With obvious sarcasm in his voice, Sanawbar said, "Please search my simple dhow, and should you find any contraband, let us make a deal: You get half and then leave me to continue my voyage to Saudi Arabia, *mio paisano.*"

Tomaino did not comprehend the mockery in Sanawbar's comment. "I am not your friend, Sanawbar, and don't ever think so. One of these days I will have the evidence to arrest you and then I will let the OVRA handle you." He ordered his Marines to search the dhow.

Sanawbar, knowing the captain's mindset, seized the moment. "*Capitano,* please allow me to escort you to the bilge; it is an ideal place to hide contraband and spies." He popped open the trap door. "Follow me."

The pungent fetidness nearly overwhelmed the suave captain neatly attired in his freshly pressed, dress-blue uniform. "Sanawbar, you have lost what little mind you have if, for a second, you believe I am going to follow you into that stinkhole." He gestured to Sanawbar to close the trap door. "Should you have contraband stashed in that purulent scupper, it would be contaminated with that God-awful stench and worth little."

They retreated to the wheelhouse and the *capitano* said earnestly, "There is a large reward for the two escaped spies: an American agent and an Italian woman traitor. I know that you would double-cross your mother, if you had one, for a few lira. Have you seen or heard of these OVRA-wanted spies? If you give me a solid tip, I might be persuaded to overlook the next few intercepts we will undoubtedly have."

Sanawbar feigned seriousness and responded, "*Capitano,* I trust you implicitly, but I know nothing of spies. I deal in hard goods, not human cargo." He smiled out of the corner of his mouth. "You know that."

The Marines entered and told the captain that they had not found any contraband or spies. He ordered them to return to the MTB. Frustrated at the scene just played out, he shook Sanawbar's hand and said, "Indeed, you are a scalawag, and in a perverse way I have some respect for you." He leaped aboard his boat, ordered the lines loosed, and shouted, "I will get you next time." To the coxswain, he commanded, "Shove off."

Sanawbar waved and shouted, "Good hunting, *mi Capitano.*"

After the Italian patrol boat had cleared the area, Sanawbar opened the trap door and helped Sofia and Walter out of the stinking bilge. Walter clutched the two backpacks close to his chest.

Sanawbar smiled crookedly at his two passengers, who were thoroughly soaked in malodorous fish carrion. He pinched his nose to tell the pair just how foul-smelling they were.

Sofia asked, "Can we go into the sea to rinse off this awful smell?"

"Of course, madam. However, I would caution you that several species of sharks lurk in these waters—the mako is particularly aggressive. And with that bloody fish smell that permeates you and your clothes, you would be an attractive banquet for this killer."

"With your help, I must chance it. I can't stand this stink and no one else could either."

Walter interjected, "Sofia, we can tough it out for another day. It is too dangerous."

"I must do it. I cannot stand my stench, or yours for that matter, *paisano*."

"If you are so determined, I will join you," Walter said in a resigned voice.

"No!" Sanawbar cried. "One at a time." He suggested, "Madame, please wait until the sunlight is stronger. Then I can stand watch with my rifle. It remains a serious risk. But if you are determined, then you must do as I say."

Later, when the early-morning light was bright, the dhow was still in the water. Sanawbar tossed a rope ladder off the stern. Sofia climbed down the ladder into the warm sea and splashed about for several minutes. "Stop splashing!" shouted Sanawbar. "You will attract the makos."

Almost on cue, Sanawbar spotted the fins of two makos beginning to circle Sofia. He shouted, "Get out!" He cycled the bolt on his rifle to load a round. "Get out now, *Signora*! Hurry! The makos are circling you."

Sofia heard the fear in his voice, and scrambled up the ladder, and jumped onto the deck. Soaking wet, but now only slightly soiled with fish odor, she shouted, "Damn! What's next? How many close calls can we endure before this odyssey is finally over?"

Walter approached to hug her. "Stay away from me, you foul smelling, rotten-fishmonger. When you smell like the Walter I know, come and hug and kiss me, but not until then. *Comprendere?*"

Sanawbar started the engine and set a course for the tip of the Arabian Peninsula. "We will move a dozen miles from here and then you, Mister Gregory, can wash in the sea." An hour later, Walter was in the Red Sea. He ducked under the shark-free water several times, and within six or seven minutes he was back on board.

Sofia cracked a crooked smile, moved toward Walter, and with exaggerated motion wiggled her nose. "I reckon you are human." She folded into his arms.

℃

Near dawn the next day, Sanawbar's dhow was several miles off the British port of Aden. A Royal Navy motor torpedo boat (MTB) challenged the dhow with its signal light. "Identify yourself."

Sanawbar responded with his signal light. "A fishing boat." Then he sent three short flashes in rapid succession, then three more short flashes, and then two long flashes—his personal recognition signal. He cut his engine to dead slow, allowing the Royal Navy boat to approach. "It would be best, Mister Gregory, if you and the Madame remain in the cabin until the Royal Navy clears us."

As the motor torpedo boat approached, the lieutenant in command shouted through his megaphone, "Is that you, you scoundrel, Sanawbar?"

Sanawbar returned the challenge, "Indeed, I am he, and I recognize your voice for the buccaneer you are, Lieutenant—ready to steal my illicit cargo. Not so?"

"Pray tell, what illegal cargo have you this morning, smuggler?"

Sanawbar matched the lieutenant's humor. "You will be sorely disappointed. There are no spoils for you. This morning I bring you two spies, escaping from the OVRA."

"Spies, you say. We can smell you from here. Perhaps they would be better off with the OVRA than on your malodorous garbage scow. Heave to. We are coming aboard."

"Very well."

The motor torpedo boat came alongside and sailors tossed lines to the dhow. The dhow's first mate made them fast. Immediately, two

Royal Marines jumped aboard the boat with their American-made 45-caliber M1 Thompson submachine guns at the ready. The sergeant snapped, "Damn, mate, I have never smelled such a rancid odor."

"Indeed. The more rancid, the less the Italians will bother me."

"Show me your cargo."

"I shall." He moved to the cabin, "Mister Gregory, and *Signora*, please come out and meet the scum of the Royal Marines."

Walter and Sofia, wearing Arab garb, emerged from the cabin with their hands up. The sergeant looked them over with a discerning eye. Pointing to Walter, he demanded, "What is your name? And who is this female?"

"I am Walter Gregory, an American citizen. I reckon that MI6 has been expecting me." He nodded toward Sofia, "This lady is *Signora* Sofia Savoy Russo, an Italian citizen under my protection."

The Marine sergeant snorted, "Is that so? We were told only about you. No dames were mentioned."

From the MTB, the lieutenant saw and heard the parlay. "Knock it off, Sergeant, and get those two people on board double quick."

Walter drew several gold certificates from his money belt and offered them to Sanawbar. With wide eyes, he grabbed them from Walter's hand. In the low light of the dawn, he looked at them carefully, and snapped them smartly against his hand. With a doleful look, he snapped, "It that all?"

Walter responded, "You are a corsair!" He gave him two more certificates. Sanawbar thanked him, "*Shokran*."

"Hurry, Sergeant. We need to get out of here before full light. We best not compromise our pirate, Sanawbar. He needs to get underway and well clear of here by first light."

The sergeant helped Walter and Sofia on board the Royal Navy MTB. As soon as the lines were loosed and secured, and the pair was seated inside the cabin, the lieutenant swung the wheel around and gunned the two powerful, Packard, marine engines. The MTB shot forward, making a huge roostertail in its wake.

The two Marines entered the cabin and offered the pair hot coffee and sweet rolls. "God!" exclaimed Sofia. "*Real* hot coffee and a sweet roll. It is an illusion. I am hallucinating." She consumed the delicacies, and a wide smile of satisfaction spread across her unkempt face. "Damn. That was delicious." She smiled at the Marine, "More, please."

Walter consumed his repast as fast as Sofia had, and nodded in assent with her to ask for another sample.

The MTB tied up at the small-boat dock at the Royal Navy Base, Aden. Standing on the dock and waiting for Walter was Commander Harmon Deering, Royal Navy, the senior MI6 agent in Aden. The MTB lieutenant ordered Walter first off. He grabbed the two backpacks and leaped onto the dock. He turned to help Sofia off. Walter turned to the crew of the MTB and shouted, "Thanks, mates. You saved our lives."

The lieutenant waved back and a large smile crept over his face. *Another job well done*, he reckoned. Even the Marines waved.

Commander Deering advanced toward Walter and Sofia and asked, "Mister Walter Gregory, I presume?" He looked at Sofia. "And, this lady must be Doctor *Signora* Sofia Savoy Russo." Without waiting for an answer, he said, "Welcome to the British Crown Colony Aden. I'm Commander Harmon Deering, the senior British intelligence officer in this area."

Sofia began to sob uncontrollably in her joy at being free at last. Walter put his left arm around her. Then he grabbed Deering's hand, shook it energetically, and with deep emotion said in a shaking voice, "My God! It is over. We are on Allied ground at long last." He continued to shake Deering's hand. "We are so very glad to see you and to know that we do not have to look over our shoulders to see if the OVRA is about to overtake us. Thank God, it's over."

Without ado, Deering rescued his hand and said, "I am here to help you." He smiled crookedly. "I must say, you two have cut quite a commotion with the 'I-ties.' Their signals are aflame with your escapades and derring-do. Never have we heard the OVRA so outraged. Rightly so, I'll add. You've had a jolly good show—at their expense. I doubt that our Special Intelligence Service chaps could have done better and returned whole."

Walter had recovered from his overwhelming joy. "What's next? First, I hope, is to help us shed these filthy disguises, quench the stench, and to remake ourselves as humans."

"Indeed so! We have made arrangements in anticipation of your needs. Follow me." The trio walked down the long quay and entered the nearby diving locker. Deering showed the pair the showers. "Inside you'll find plenty of hot water, soap, shampoo, scrub brushes, toothbrushes and paste, towels, and bathrobes."

Sofia commented, "You are an angel."

Walter remained silent, but did notice that at almost every corner, armed Marines were at the ready.

Deering saw that Walter had noticed the Marines. "You two are high-profile characters, so we have laid on extra security to ensure that nothing happens to you 'spies.'" He continued, "Leave those foul rags in the receptacle. Empty your backpacks, dump them in the receptacle, rinse off what items you can, and place them in the two gripsacks on the bench. Take your time. We have a full day for you."

Sometime later, the pair exited the showers well-scrubbed and odor-free, and dressed in comfortable robes. Deering led them to a waiting sedan. The driver opened the rear door for Walter and Sofia. Deering took the passenger seat. "We're headed for the VIP Officer's Quarters."

On arrival, he said, "*Signora,* your lodging is on the right. Gregory, yours is on the left. Some people will arrive shortly to help you."

Within the next few hours, various service people arrived at their quarters: a barber for Walter, a beautician for Sofia, and a storekeeper with naval uniforms without insignias for the pair. A couple of the nurses donated various lingerie items for Sofia. Delightfully pleased, she examined the treasures and exclaimed, "Can this be true? Have I returned to civilization?"

Later that afternoon, the refreshed Walter and Sofia were in a cement-block room with no windows located deep in an anonymous warehouse. Two armed Marines guarded the outside door. Deering and two of his MI6 agents were prepared to debrief the pair. However, he was concerned that Sofia did not have a security clearance, especially for the code-word Gamma intelligence program.

Walter said, "*Signora* Russo is cleared for whatever level is necessary. She has been with me all the way. We would not be here without her resolve, dedication, and superior skills. *Signora* Russo is a gallant woman, and I vouch wholeheartedly for her. *Capisci?*"

Commander Deering stared at Walter with steady, cold, and enigmatic eyes. "Then, Mister Gregory you take full responsibility for *Signora* Russo's trustworthiness?"

Walter snapped, "Of course." Then, to ease the tension, he said in a milder voice, "The matter is settled. Let's get on with it."

"Very well," Deering said. "Let's proceed."

He stood and said in his most professional voice, "Mister Gregory and *Signora* Russo, understand wholeheartedly that everything said and seen in this debriefing about your escapade in Italian East Africa is classified Top Secret, Special Access Intelligence." He looked at the pair with hard, steady eyes. "Do you understand?"

Walter responded, "Yes, of course."

Sofia grabbed Walter's arm. "I don't understand. What is he saying?"

Walter put both of his hands on her shoulders, looked at her with empathetic eyes. "This debriefing is super secret, and we have a special obligation to keep to ourselves what we hear and see in this debriefing."

With a puzzled look, Sofia said, "That's curious. We've experienced this adventure and we know all there is to know."

Slightly flustered, Walter said, "True. Say, 'Yes,' please."

With finality, Sofia announced, "Yes."

With firm resolve, Commander Deering said, "Understand, any unauthorized disclosure of the intelligence discussed in this room will result in severe judicial penalties. Crystal clear?"

The pair nodded in the affirmative.

"Very well. Sign these Official Secret Act documents and we'll continue."

It took a minute or two for the pair to complete the signing procedure.

Deering retrieved the documents and placed them in his briefcase.

"First, I must tell you that you two are the most wanted fugitives on the planet. The 'bad guys' have flooded the world with reward posters and shortwave radio announcements to get you two notorious blackguards, dead or alive. The amount of funds being offered is staggering in these Depression times. Our cryptographers have discerned that every dictatorial government in the world has their agents looking for you two: the OVRA, Gestapo, Cheka, the Spanish CESIS, Japan's Black Dragons, and even the Vatican's 'The Entity.' In addition, I'm ashamed to say that some of our 'friends' also are anxious to find you."

Walter said with resignation, "Worldwide recognition as an American spy is about the last thing I need. There goes my international geophysical and wildcat oil business." Then, nonchalantly, he added, "What the hell? I'll concentrate on domestic oil production."

Deering continued, "Through our radio intercept programs we have confirmation that most of these hostile intelligence outfits now know that you are here at this naval base in Aden."

Sofia, perplexed, asked, "I don't understand. We have only been here a day and a half. How can they know about us?"

"We have several foreign agents working on this base, and with all the folderol surrounding your arrival, it was inevitable that you would be spotted and they would communicate with their controllers. We have their intercepts."

Puzzled, Sofia stared at Deering and burst forth, "That's insane. Why didn't you arrest these agents as soon as you identified them?"

"Madame Russo," he replied with some irritation in his voice, "We let these agents alone for several reasons. Our counterintelligence officers know who they are, what they are doing, and when they do it. If we were to arrest these people, another batch of unknown agents would soon be here. We'd have to start at ground zero to ferret them out, and no telling how long that would take, or how much intelligence they might gather before we identified them."

Sofia, somewhat chagrined, said, "Thank you, Commander Deering. I should have known better. My apologies."

Deering said, "Let's begin." He turned to their court reporter, a yeoman first-class, and said, "Log the time and date, those present, and the rest of the relevant prologue information."

Deering told Walter that MI6 would send a copy of their brief in toto via back-channel radio communications to the Intelligence and Research Bureau of the State Department. As the pair's story unfolded, Deering asked to see the evidence Walter had collected. Reluctantly, he agreed.

Deering commented, "You have three phosgene canisters. Please leave one for us. We will not outmaneuver your State Department in whatever they want to do with them at the League of Nations. We want our scientists to run tests on it to confirm what was in it. And we would like to have one of those radioactive shards."

As a gesture of good will, and clearly without permission, Walter agreed. He determined it was the least he could do to acknowledge the life-saving help the British government had provided to them, and to ensure future affable cooperation. The debriefing extended to 2200 hours. Earlier, a steward had brought sandwiches and tea for dinner.

Finally, Walter and Sofia returned to their quarters and slept soundly, assured that Marine guards were posted.

೮෨

Shortly after dawn the next morning, Commander Deering escorted Walter and Sofia into the secure room. "Last night, our cryptographers intercepted and decoded several OVRA electronic transmissions confirming that they will take aggressive action to stop you from reaching a friendly democracy. In the past twelve hours, six Italian aircraft have over-flown this naval base. We launched a section of Gloster Gladiators to intercept them, but there was no contact."

Walter was disgusted. "I thought we were safe here under British protection. Will this odyssey never end?"

"We are going to get you to Port Said safely. You can count on it." He smiled and his eyes flashed with devilry. "We have set up a ruse." He paused to refer to a notecard. "Earlier this morning, we sent a coded message to the intelligence section of the First Lord of the Admiralty, in a code that we know the OVRA cryptographers have broken. We said we are sending you two to Sallâh, on the Indian Ocean coast in Oman, in our Blackburn Perth Flying Boat. And, from there, an American submarine would take you on board."

Deering paused to catch his breath and to evaluate the reaction of his charges. Satisfied, he continued. "To mislead the spies on this base, we're tasking one of our officers and one of our nurses to impersonate the two of you boarding that Flying Boat. We'll make a small to do with armed Marine guards. I'll shake the impersonators' hands and bid them *adieu*."

Walter cocks his head and comments, "Impressive. I'm delighted we're allies."

Deering cracked a small smile.

"A section of three Gloster Gladiator fighters will escort the Flying Boat for about two hundred miles of the five-hundred-mile trip: far enough to fend off any *Regia Aeronautica Italiana* aircraft attempting to intercept the Flying Boat and shoot it down."

He continued, "We will bring you to Port Said. From there, you will board an American heavy cruiser bound for Norfolk, Virginia."

Walter reflected for a few seconds. "An ingenious stratagem. How confident are you that the Italians will take the bait?"

"We don't give away all our secrets, Mister Gregory. Be assured one hundred percent that the Italians have acted on our false message. Even as we speak, six Fiat CR 32 fighter aircraft have been serviced and armed, and the pilots briefed on their mission."

Sofia commented, "You people do deserve your reputation. Remarkable."

Deering continued, "There is more. In another Admiralty low-level code that the Italians have broken, we posted a ship's movement notice. Today, a squadron of three destroyers is sailing for our ship-yard in Port Said for routine maintenance."

ఴ

By mid-afternoon, Walter and Sofia were on board the Royal Navy destroyer *HMS Codrington* sailing north in the Red Sea for the 1,500 mile, four-day journey through the Suez Canal to Port Said on the Mediterranean Sea.

ఴ

Looming in the moonlight was the massive American heavy cruiser *USS Houston* at anchor off Port Said. A motor launch approached the gangway of the cruiser. The British coxswain shouted through his megaphone to the *Houston's* Officer of the Deck, "Ahoy, *Houston*. I have two passengers for your ship. Permission to come aboard, sir."

"Identify yourself."

"His Majesty's ship *Codrington* out of the British Crown Colony Aden."

"Very well." He drew his Colt 45 pistol. "Standby." After a short pause, two Marine guards appeared on the quarterdeck with their M1 Thompson 45 submachine guns. The Officer of the Deck shouted at the coxswain, "Permission granted."

Walter and Sofia scrambled up the long ladder with their gripsacks and greeted the Officer of the Deck. He told them to stand by and called the bridge on the M1 telephone system to notify the Captain that the passengers were on board.

The Captain ordered, "Weigh anchor." Within the minute, the boatswain mates from the Special Sea and Anchor Detail engaged the powerful windlass to haul in the anchor. A few seconds later, the Captain ordered the lee helmsman, "Dead slow ahead."

The able-bodied seaman responded, "Dead slow ahead, aye, Sir." He quickly moved the twin handles on the engine-order telegraph to their stops; its bells rang loudly, and he then moved the handles to the DEAD SLOW AHEAD position.

The Chief Engineer acknowledged the bridge's order, and shouted instructions to the boiler-tender seamen.

The mighty quad marine screws began to turn and the USS Houston moved forward; slowly at first, but soon its bow was slicing through the seas and its fantail was leaving a sparkling wake.

Lieutenant Michael Schoppe, the ship's intelligence officer, greeted the pair, and asked a few personal questions to confirm their identities. Satisfied, he said, "I'm sending a message to the Office of Naval Intelligence for forwarding to the National Command Authority, "Mission accomplished."

The next morning, the Houston was steaming westward at eighteen knots in the Mediterranean Sea. Walter and Sofia strolled the aft deck.

"Sofia, we've had an incredible adventure. Throughout, you have been a no-nonsense, take-charge, wisecracking, wonderful woman with a copious lot of brassbound nerve." He looked deeply into Sofia's eyes, took both of her hands, and said, "I realize that you cannot return to Italy." He asked with a slight hint of a taunt,

"Shall I have the Captain dock at the Knights Templar pier in Malta for you to debark, perhaps at Casablanca? How about the Canary Islands, or St. Helena, to contemplate Napoleon Bonaparte's military career?"

Sofia turned away for a second, then looked at Walter with soft tears in her eyes and a tantalizing smile. "Walter Gregory, how about Odessa, Texas?"

"Deal! *Signora, mi amore.*"

author's notes

I have based this yarn in the aftermath of the **Second Italian-Abyssinian War** (1935-1936).

On 3 October 1935, El Duce, **Benito Mussolini,** dictator of Italy, ordered **General Rodolfo Graziani** to launch an invasion of Abyssinia from Italian Somaliland and Eritrea. The Italian fascist army of 100,000 men, with an array of modern weapons, swarmed across the border into Abyssinia's Tigray Province.

The Emperor of Abyssinia, the Conquering Lion of Judah, **Haile Selassie**, declared war on Italy and issued his compelling mobilization order:

"All men able to carry a spear go to Addis Ababa. Every married man will bring his wife to cook and wash for him. Every unmarried man will bring any unmarried woman he can find to cook and wash for him. Women with babies, the blind, and those too aged to carry a spear are excused. Anyone who is qualified for battle and is found at home after receiving this order will be hanged."

The primitive Abyssinia Army fought bravely, but was unable to overcome the Italians' contemporary weapons: tanks, machine guns, attack aircraft, and chemical weapons contained in special artillery shells and dropped in canisters from *Regia Aeronautica Italiana* bombers.

The Italians' use of chemical weapons was in clear violation of the League of Nations Covenant, Article X, 1925, which banned the use of poison gas. The "terrible rain that burned and killed" demoralized the Ethiopians and was instrumental in their defeat.

Axum. This is the Abyssinian city in which the characters are based. It is a holy city and was the center of the Kingdom of Aksum. King Ezana introduced Christianity in Abyssinia in the fourth century. Around Axum, obelisks (stele) are used to mark the royal burial chambers. The Church of Our Lady Mary of Zion houses the Biblical Ark of the Covenant in which are the Tablets of Law (the Ten Commandments).

Miscellaneous information. Modern Ethiopians claim to be direct descendants of the Queen of Sheba. In 1936, the language of Abyssinia was a native Amharic derivative.

Organization for Vigilance and Repression of Anti-Fascism. (OVRA) This outfit was the fascist Italian secret police. It is usually referred to by its initials: OVRA. The fascist dictator Benito Mussolini formed the OVRA in 1927 after an attempt on his life. He appointed Arturo Bocchine as its head. Approximately 5,000 OVRA agents infiltrated all aspects of life in Italy and its colonies. The OVRA charter was to stop anti-fascist activity or sentiment; to control and prevent political dissent; and to arrest, try in rump trials, and convict persons they accused of being "enemies of the State." Their courts sentenced those convicted to harsh prison terms or death.

Cyrenaica. Italy defeated the Ottoman Empire in the war of 1911 to 1912 and occupied the Turks' North African colonies of Cyrenaica, Fezzan, and Tripolitania. During the 1920s, rebels under the leadership of **Emir Omar Mukhtar** waged a fierce guerilla campaign for independence. In 1931, the Italian Army captured Mukhtar and hanged him, effectively ending the rebel campaign. In 1929, the Italian government combined these three colonies to form Libya.

Werner Heisenberg (1901–1976) received th e Nobel Prize in Physics in 1932. He was a German theoreti cal physicist and one of the key creators of quantum mechanics. In 1927, he published his famous uncertainty principle, for which he is best known. In 1939, shortly after the discovery of nuclear fission, he joined the German nuclear energy project, known as the "Uranium Club." He became the principal scientist in this Club. He focused his research on the development of sustained nuclear fission—a chain reaction to be used to develop an atomic bomb. The essential chemical element needed for this re-search was an isotope of uranium with the atomic number of 235.

The uranium project was sponsored and funded by Albert Speer (1905–1981), Minister of Armaments and War Production for the Third Reich.

Heisenberg visited the University of Michigan in June and July of 1939 to give lectures on nuclear physics. He was offered the opportunity to defect to the United States, but he declined.

Albert Einstein (1878–1955) was awarded the Nobel Prize in Physics in 1921. He was renowned for his development of the relativity theory and research into theoretical physics. In August 1939, he sent a letter to President Roosevelt detailing progress in developing a nuclear chain reaction using the 235 isotope of uranium, which, it was hoped, would release "vast amounts of energy." Nuclear scientists at the University of Chicago, and in France, Italy, and in the Third Reich, were also conducting such research. In the near future, one of these groups of researchers would become successful. This success would lead to the development of an atomic bomb that would obliterate an entire city.

Enrico Fermi (1901–1978) earned the Nobel Prize in Physics in 1938. He was an Italian theoretical physicist noted for his contributions to the development of quantum theory, nuclear and particle physics, and statistical mechanics. He immigrated to the USA in 1939 and worked on the development of the atomic bomb at the University of Chicago.

photographic gallery

I have posted the following photographs in the order in which each subject was first mentioned.

Prologue

Italian Savoy flag

Abyssinian flag

Chapter One

Savoia-Marchetti SM-79, *Regia Aeronautica Italiana*

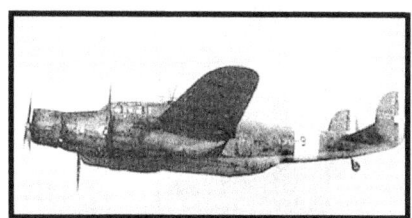

CANT Z.1007, *Regia Aeronautica Italiana*

186

Benito Mussolini (1881 to 1945); "Il Duce," the fascist dictator of Italy from 1922 to 1943 and leader of the National Fascist Party

Victor Emmanuel Savoy III (1869 to 1947); King of the Italian Socialist Republic

Fasces

Omar Mukhtar Mukhtar (1862 to 1931); Arab leader of guerrillas in Italian-occupied Cyrenaica

Generale Rodolfo Graziani (1882 to 1955); First Viceroy and Governor General of Italian East Africa, and Marshal of the Italian army in East Africa

Chapter Two

Lockheed Model 10 Electra

Pan American Sikorsky Flying Boat Model VS-44

General Francisco Franco (1892 to 1975); head of the Falangists Party and leader of the revolution against the Marxists' Spanish government

Colonel Theodore "Teddy" Roosevelt (1858 to 1919); the 26th President of the U.S. In the Spanish-American war, Roosevelt led the "Rough Riders" in their charge up San Juan Hill, 1898.

President Sam Houston (1793 to 1863); leader of the Texas Revolution and President of the Republic of Texas from 1836 to 1838, and 1841 to 1844

General John J "Black Jack" Pershing (1860 to 1948); leader of the American military expedition to capture the Mexican bandit Pancho Villa and General of the American Armies in France from 1917 to 1918

Francisco "Pancho" Villa (1878 to 1923), Mexican revolutionary led his gang into Columbus, New Mexico and murdered several American citizens

Chapter Three

Shepheard's Hotel

Cairo Museum

SS Rex Italia

Chapter Four

4x5 Graflex camera

Enrico Fermi, Ph.D. (1901 to 1954); Nobel Laureate Physics, 1938, Physics Professor of Theoretical Physics at the University of Rome, and the University of Chicago.

Werner Heisenberg, Ph.D. (1901 to 1976); Nobel Laureate, Physics 1932. Ordinarius Professor of Physics, University of Leipzig. Nuclear physicist in Berlin during WorldWar II

Albert Speer (1905 to 1961); Minister of Armaments and War Production for the Third Reich

Admiral Wilhelm Canaris (1897 to 1945); head of the Nazis' Abwehr, German military intelligence.

Chapter Five

Honorable Cordell Hull, Esq.
(1871 to 1955); Secretary of
State from 1933 to 1944; Nobel
Laureate, Peace Prize 1945

President Franklin Delano
Roosevelt (1882 to 1945); 32nd
President of the U.S. (1933 to
1945); concerned that the Third
Reich (Nazi Germany) would
develop an atomic bomb

Harry Hopkins (1890 to 1946);
President Roosevelt's chief diplomatic advisor and troubleshooter

Boeing YB-17, Flying Fortress

Chapter Six

Gian Galeazzo Ciano (1903 to 1944); Minister of Foreign Affairs in the fascist government of Italy; Benito Mussolini's son-in-law

Pan American World Airways Transatlantic Flying Boat

Imperial Airways Short Empire Flying Boat

Imperial Airways Handley Page H.P.45

Chapter Eight

Beretta 32 Pistol

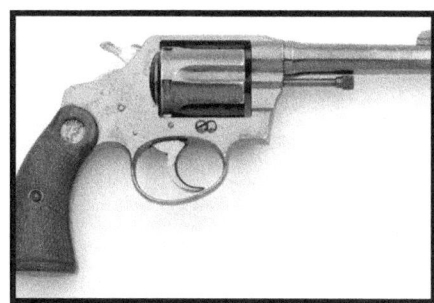

Colt 38 Special Pistol

Beretta 38 Pistol

Nubian Ibex

Vixen

Early Leica camera

Chapter Fifteen

Savoia-Marchetti, SM-79

Fiat CR.32

Chapter Seventeen

Chapter Eighteen

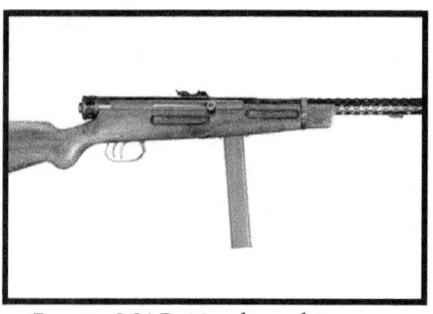

Beretta MAB-38 submachine gun

Dhow

Chapter Seventeen

Italian Motor Torpedo Boat, MTB

British Motor Torpedo Boat, MTB

USS Houston

Author's Notes

Haile Selassie (1892 to 1975);
Emperor of Abyssinia from 1930
to 1974. Known as "The Lion
of Judah," he rallied worldwide
support for his resistance to the
Italian invasion in 1935.

about the author

Captain Shelton is retired from active and reserve U.S. Navy service. He attended the Naval School of Photography and documented Navy and Marine Corps activities in Korea, French Indochina, and other areas in the Western Pacific. Commissioned as a Photographic Officer, he then served in Vietnam and other Pacific regions.

Shelton earned his Master of Arts Degree (Cinema) at the University of Southern California. For thirty years, he produced a host of information and documentary motion-media shows, winning over forty awards in national and international film competitions and festivals. His peers elected him a Fellow of both the Information Film Producers of America and the Society for Technical Communication. He served as the President of the Information Film Producers of America.

Shelton has published extensively in trade magazines, peer-reviewed journals, and commercial publications. His professional book, *Communicating Ideas with Film, Video, and Multimedia,* garnered the Best of Show award in the Society for Technical Communication's Spotlight Publication Competition.

Currently, he is writing historical novels whose *mise en scène* is the Far East and Africa. His action-adventure novel *St. Catherine's Crown*, published in 2013, garnered wide acclaim from reviewers. The narrative is set during the Russian Revolution. Following the regicide of the royal family, the harrowing post-Revolution adventures of Grand Duchess Anastasia and her cousin Lieutenant Kirik Pirogoff begin, as they travel the Trans-Siberian Railroad to refuge in northwestern China.

Details regarding his literary work are posted on his web site, **sheltoncomm.com**.

www.ingramcontent.com/pod-product-compliance
Lightning Source LLC
Chambersburg PA
CBHW072053170626
46813CB00004B/1335